WOLF'S CANDLE

**Center Point
Large Print**

**This Large Print Book carries the
Seal of Approval of N.A.V.H.**

DANE COOLIDGE

WOLF'S CANDLE

CENTER POINT PUBLISHING
THORNDIKE, MAINE

This Center Point Large Print edition
is published in the year 2003 by arrangement with
Golden West Literary Agency.

The text of this Large Print edition is unabridged. In other
aspects, this book may vary from the original edition. Printed in
Thailand. Set in 16-point Times New Roman type by
Bill Coskrey and Gary Socquet.

ISBN 1-58547-322-7

Library of Congress Cataloging-in-Publication Data.

Coolidge, Dane, 1873-1940.
  Wolf's candle / Dane Coolidge.--Center Point large print ed.
    p. cm.
  ISBN 1-58547-322-7 (lib. bdg. : alk. paper)
   1. Large type books. I. Title.

PS3505.O5697W65 2003

2003043531

CONTENTS

SPOILING THE PHILISTINES

LIBERTY AND JUSTICE

WAR

THE AFTERMATH

SPOILING THE PHILISTINES

CHAPTER I

THE WOLF'S WAY

DOWN THE DEEP-WORN TRAIL from the north John Fox rode into the Hot Country; while before him, like waves before the prow of a ship, the man-killer lizards fled. On both sides, a wall of thorns, the giant cacti hedged him in; and he passed beneath the wands of slender *ocatillas,* whose pendant lanterns light the way for the wolf. They burned red as blood in the smiting midday sun casting long, black shadows across his path—but Don Juan did not believe in signs. With his rifle across his lap he dared the gods to turn him back until he had spoiled the Philistines.

North Pass had a bad name, and the graves to show for it, and as the pack train passed a sagging cross, each muleteer cast a stone on the mound. It was the Mexican way of offering up a prayer for the soul of one suddenly killed. This man had been dead a long time, for his pile of stones was high—there were others not ten prayers deep.

Mal Paso, the place was called, for down it came venturesome Americans and bandits returning from forays—but John Fox was a man of peace. Behind him in a long train sixty pack mules grunted and groaned beneath the weight of their loads of sewing machines, and in every Mexican house where there was money to pay the woman would buy a *máquina.*

He was a little man with high cheek-bones and a tawny, bristling mustache; a man weighted down with pistols; a man with deep-set eyes that searched out every shadow— but with it all only a vender of sewing machines. Behind him and on foot followed a sun-blackened Yaqui Indian, searching the dust for enemy tracks; while the muleteers all carried, beside their long-lashed *tapaojos,* a rifle in the hand. They were fighters, every one; but their *patron* sold sewing machines—to women.

The trail widened out, other trails joined in where cattle had come down from the hills. Along the sandy washes they lay chewing their cuds, their noses cruelly decorated with the cactus-joints they ate, but placid, well-fed, calm. Woodpeckers squawked from their holes in the giant cactus; doves hurtled past, flying low; and on the dry, sun-baked wind there came a smell of cool water and green things growing in swamps. Then under the edge of the high mesa Fox came suddenly on Miraflores, a white house hidden away among the palms.

There were broad fields of corn, long rows of sugar cane, the dark green of mangoes and tamarinds; and, thrust against the sky on stems as slender as straws, the delicately tufted tops of coco palms. The red-tiled house was long with a corredor in front and the thatched huts of the servants beyond but, beneath the shade of clustered trees, it was sunk in midday sleep. Yet as he reined in his horse and looked at the ranch-house Don Juan saw something that moved. Something red, patterned in black like a ladybird's wings. It stepped forth, became a woman, and was gone.

"Fidel!" he called, as his Yaqui tracker came up, "who

lives here? What is this place?"

Fidel removed his palm-leaf hat and fixed the Boss with his one good eye.

"Don Francisco Gallardo," he answered respectfully. "He is a Spaniard and very rich. It is said that in three days a man on a good horse can hardly ride around his land. And where those palms are, there rises a great spring that irrigates all these fields."

"Enough!" responded the Boss. "Rest the mules in the shade. I will sell them a sewing machine."

He spurred Pardo, his spirited gray, down the rocky slope and washed in the tepid stream before the mules came down to drink. Then in the shade of a spreading tamarind he opened up his war-bag and began a careful toilette. First he brushed the dust from his slim, high-heeled boots and polished his silver spurs; then he pulled off his soiled shirt and slipped on another one, knotting a red silk handkerchief at his throat. He brushed back the tawny hair that stood up like a lion's mane and parted it sleekly to the side; and as a last, dainty lure to win the feminine heart he touched his red mustache with perfume.

The black Yaqui grunted, the muleteers spat in the dirt as he mounted and rode up towards the house; but Fox cared nothing for them. The whole Gallardo family had gathered on the porch to witness the passage of his pack train and when he lowered one bar and jumped his horse over the rest, it was seen he was *bien jinete,* a horseman as good as the best. He swung lower and picked up the bar, putting it back with a dexterous fling, but when he looked again she was gone. The girl with the red silk dress, patterned in black like a ladybird's wing.

She had retired with her mother, as custom decreed, and the two young men were not far behind. Servants crowded the kitchen door, their eyes big at the sight of him with his fine mount and silver-braided sombrero, and when he laid his glove-whitened hand on the swinging gate the old man bade him enter.

"Pase! Pase! Señor!" he called, advancing to meet him; and Fox doffed his hat and bowed.

"I am Juan Fox," he said, with American directness. "Have I the honor of addressing Don Francisco Gallardo?"

"Your humble servant," responded the old Don, shaking hands. "Pray consider my poor house your own."

"A thousand thanks," returned Don Juan. "It is indeed a beautiful place and blessed with a charming master, but as it is far to Todos Santos and my mules are under the packs I will state my business at once."

"Please do so, if you must," replied the Don, leading the way into the spacious corredor. "We poor country people are always glad when strangers stop, but it is three leagues to the town and your mules are heavily loaded. Is it some kind of machinery you carry?"

"Yes, sir," answered Fox, twisting his lips into a wry smile. "I am selling sewing machines."

"What?" cried Don Francisco, rising suddenly from the rawhide chair into which he had just settled his bulk; and his blue eyes which before had beamed so hospitably became suddenly narrowed and chilled.

"Yes—sewing machines," repeated Juan, his face set; and Gallardo regarded him shrewdly. He was a stout man, with a curly beard and a perfect set of white teeth which however no longer flashed a welcome. He frowned and shook his head at the thought.

"But that is something for women!" he protested. "I thought you had machinery for some mine."

"No," returned the American, "I sell *máquinas de coser.* And though it is late I stopped for a minute to see if your wife would buy one."

"Carai!" exclaimed Gallardo, ignoring the hint, "there is something strange about this. But wait—what else do you do?"

"When their eyes are bad I sell the ladies glasses. It makes it easier to sew."

"Ha, ha!" laughed the old man, suddenly recovering his spirits. "You are a rare person—an American, I know. And what else do you do?"

He fixed the young man with a quizzical smile and Fox could hear a movement in the darkened room to which the ladies had retired, but his poker face never changed.

"If anyone is ill," he said, "I give them medicine. But only when no doctor is near."

"Muy bien," nodded Gallardo. "And what else?"

"Well—" and the American grinned—"I sometimes look at mines."

"Ah! Aha!" cried Don Francisco triumphantly. "At last I have found you out. You do not look like a man to peddle sewing machines to women."

"Nevertheless," replied Fox, "that is my business. Have I your permission to show one to the Señora?"

"To be sure—if she wishes," responded Gallardo, still

laughing; and clapped his hands for a servant.

An Indian maid came running, pop-eyed with excitement, and Juan glanced back at the kitchen door. The gawking faces of the women were distorted with suppressed laughter, but at his look they ducked out of sight.

"Send your mistress," ordered the old Don and as the girl went into the cloistered rooms Fox made a brief signal to his men. Then as if by magic two muleteers came hurrying in with a sewing machine between them. It was new and shining, complete in every part and ready for the demonstrator to begin. He drew up a chair, pulled some fabrics from a drawer and at a stroke of the hand raised the presser foot and slipped in two pieces of cloth. He gave the balance wheel a flip, started the treadle with his feet and in an instant had begun to sew.

Standing over him Don Francisco hardly noticed when his wife stepped through the door, but Fox rose quickly to his feet. He bowed gravely, met her eyes and bowed again, then sat down and went on with his work. It was seldom that the wives of rich *hacendados* wished a sewing machine peddler to be presented. He shoved the cotton aside, laid down a strip of silk and—along its edge—a filmy piece of lace; then he slipped in a small attachment, clamped down on the hem and sewed with lightning speed. A moment later he took out the bit of silk with the dainty lace attached.

"Ah! How beautiful!" exclaimed the Señora; but the demonstration had only begun. He hemmed, he tucked, he ruffled and plaited; until at last with a special attachment he embroidered a gorgeous flower, and rose with another low bow.

"I am only a mechanic," he said, "to demonstrate the machine. Will the lady not try it herself?"

For a moment Doña Luz hesitated, sorely tempted by the mechanism and the array of silken fabrics spread out, but determined to make a good trade. Then she sighed helplessly and shook her head.

"My poor eyes!" she exclaimed. "I cannot see the thread." But at the words he held up his hand. A minute later a muleteer came running with a box full of spectacles and lenses.

"Try these," he suggested, picking out a pair of glasses, and with a cry of delight the Señora clapped them on until at last she found one that fitted.

"These are good—these are perfect!" she said. "But how much is the price?"

"That makes no difference," spoke up her husband, smiling. "Take them, Luz—and the *máquina,* too."

"Ah, no, no!" she protested. "It will be too much, I know. But I need these to read my prayers."

"They are twenty-five pesos," stated Fox. "But with a sewing machine only ten."

"Ten!" she shrilled. "And how much is the machine?"

"Two hundred pesos as it stands, with a hundred assorted needles and this book of instructions thrown in. By reading it carefully you can learn every—"

"Two hundred!" she repeated, her black eyes turning agate; but Don Juan knew the ways of her kind. The thrifty Spanish wives of wealthy ranchers who make a virtue of saving every centavo.

"For poor people," he suggested, "I have another, not so good, which I sell for seventy-five pesos."

"We will take this one," announced Don Francisco magnificently.

"But I cannot learn to run it!" cried the Señora in despair. "So many parts! So many things to do!"

"Sit down," said Fox, "and I will show you." And he drew up a chair beside her. "First lift this—then put in the cloth—turn this wheel—then start the treadle."

Doña Luz tried her best for a minute. Then, still intent upon driving a bargain, she threw up her hands and quit.

"I cannot learn!" she wailed. "It is this thing below. I will take the glasses—that is all."

"Very well," answered Juan, "they are twenty-five pesos." And he signaled for the muleteers to come.

"But you said ten!" charged the Señora angrily.

"With the machine," he corrected and glanced at Don Francisco.

"That is true," he agreed. "But a little moment, my friend. I wish my wife to have this *máquina*."

"I cannot run it!" cried Doña Luz spitefully. "And two hundred is entirely too much."

"I am a Yanqui," replied Fox, "and a one-price man. Also the hour is late."

He motioned to the machine, but as the *mozos* caught it up Gallardo raised his hand.

"Elodia!" he called. "Come here, my darling!"

There was a rustle behind the half-door, the clack of Cuban heels and the Ladybird darted out, radiant. She glanced at Don Juan first, then at her mother and the machine which she had admired so long from afar, and last of all at her father.

"Can you learn to run this *máquina?*" he asked. "Then

do so and it is yours."

"I will try," she said, smiling daringly at Fox; and he answered the look in her eyes.

CHAPTER II

"THEY CALL THEMSELVES MEN!"

TO SELL SEWING MACHINES it was sometimes necessary to flirt and Don Juan knew the signs. Elodia stood before him a little shyly, but made up to show every charm. She was a dazzling brunette with all the tropic colors of the ladybird—dark hair with a gleam of red, deep black eyes with that look he knew and the silken legs of a Spanish dancer. She was supple, she was tall, and her robe of China silk was the color of a ladybird's wing. Fox looked again to be sure there was no mistake and she blushed to her pulsating throat.

"Sit here," he said, bowing low; and in his ruthless blue eyes there burned the lambent flame of the admiring, predatory male. Without a glance at her mother, who stood sternly by her spouse, he drew another chair up beside her and started the balance wheel.

"Turn it towards you," he directed, "then pump with your feet until you learn how the treadle works."

"Yes," she answered dutifully and in the long silence that followed Doña Luz retired in a huff. They were left alone, except for the staring eyes that regarded them from behind half-closed doors, but Don Juan was discretion itself. For the daughter of the house—and with that look in her eyes—to be left with him even for a moment was almost unbelievable in Mexico; and Elodia was undoubtedly a flirt. She trailed a wisp of fragrant hair across his smooth-shaven cheek and their heads drew closer as they worked.

The lesson went on apace, she was learning fast, and as their hands happened to meet she glanced up at him, smiling. His hands were small and white, almost as slender as her own, but full-muscled, sinewy, masculine; and at every touch as he deftly turned the wheels she felt the fire of passion.

"You are bold," she said at last, but without looking up. "Are you holding my hand on purpose?"

"No, no," he protested jocularly. "But if I did, then who could blame me? Your beauty has turned my head."

She slapped his hand playfully and leaned her head closer and as his perfumed mustache swept across her cheek he whispered in her ear,

"Do not learn so fast, my Mariquita. In a few more minutes I must go."

A wave of silent laughter passed over her lithe form.

"You are bold," she said again. "But why am I your Mariquita?"

"You are colored like one," he whispered, "the little good-luck ladybird that leads us all to happiness. All red and black and burnished brown. Are you never lonely, hidden away in this house among the palms?"

"Never lonely," she repeated, "because I am never alone. Have you no fear for those who watch us?"

Fox looked up quickly, suddenly aware of a presence and, above the half-door of the room, he beheld a face that startled him. The man was tall and handsome with curly brown hair; but there was a cast in one eye, a sinister squint, that made Juan's bold heart miss a beat.

"Who is that?" he demanded, pretending to adjust the thread. "Is he your husband? Is he jealous?"

"Be careful," she warned, "or he will kill you. He is my brother—I am not married."

"No?" he exclaimed with a dare-devil smile. "Are there no men, then, in this country?"

"They call themselves men!" she answered bitterly; and sewed a long, straight line. "Enough!" she said, "I have learned my lesson. It is time for you to go."

She rose as her father came out another door with a heavy bag of money in his hand, but Fox had taken courage.

"I will go when I am ready," he replied. "Your brother is nothing to me."

Elodia gazed at him a moment, then stood by the machine while her father came over, smiling.

"Have you learned to sew, already?" he beamed. "Then we must pay Señor Fox and let him go."

He set the bag of silver on the table and spilled out half the coins.

"Count them," he invited. "There are two hundred and ten pesos—for the glasses and my daughter's machine."

"Many thanks," replied Juan, scooping the flood of money back, "if you have counted them, that is enough."

"But my friend," protested Gallardo, laughing indulgently, "perhaps I have counted them wrong!"

"No difference," answered Fox with a smile and a careless shrug. "What is a dollar or so, between friends?"

He held up his hand for Fidel, and the Yaqui came

on the run.

"Take these pesos," he said, "and put them in the pack. And tell the *arrieros* we will go."

"*Sí, Señor,*" replied the Indian and as he went back to the mules Don Francisco laughed again.

"You trust him?" he asked. "This black Yaqui! I have heard that the Americanos think of nothing but money. What is to keep him from stealing a few pesos?"

"This!" responded Juan, touching the pistol on his hip; and the Don showed all his white teeth.

"For a little man," he said, "you are *bravo*."

"Am I little?" demanded Fox, "with this on? When Colonel Colt invented the six-shooter he made all men the same size."

"Ah! True!" nodded Gallardo. "I had not thought of that. I had not thought of you as a fighting man. But before you go, here is something I wish to show you." And he drew a huge watch from his pocket.

"Señor Fox," he began, "here is a watch that is very old. I have had it for many years, until now it will run no longer. Please look inside and see if you can fix it—I will pay you well if you do."

Don Juan looked down the lane to where his mules were beginning to move, and snapped open the heavy silver case. Then with a prospector's lens he examined the gummed wheels, shook it lightly and handed it back.

"It could be fixed," he said, "if I had the time. But already I have stayed too long."

"Send the mules on ahead!" urged the old man impulsively. "I have something of importance to discuss. And when you go, take this watch along and mend it. It was my father's—made in France."

"Very well," agreed Fox; but as he reached out to take it he met the eyes of Doña Luz, standing behind.

"And how much will it be?" she asked.

"Oh, nothing," he answered carelessly. "I shall be very glad to do it for my friend."

He bowed to the smiling Don and was tucking the watch away when the half-door behind him was kicked violently open and for the first time the brothers appeared. Bizco, the elder, strode swiftly across the corredor, a sinister gleam in his mismatched eyes.

"Give it back!" he commanded harshly. "The watch!"

"To be sure," replied Fox. "Here it is, Don Francisco. *Adios, Señoras—adios!*"

He bowed formally to the ladies and was turning to leave when Manuel, the younger brother, leapt forward.

"There is the road!" he cried. "Now go!"

"To be sure!" returned Juan again. "And why not?"

He paused, bristling angrily, and looked him over from head to foot. But before he could speak there was a roar from Gallardo that made both brothers jump.

"Begone!" he shouted, catching first one and then the other and flinging them violently aside. "I am the head of this house and I order *you* to leave! This gentleman is my guest."

He glared at them so menacingly that they rushed back through the doorway, quickly followed by the frightened women, and a sudden silence fell.

"Now, my friend," went on the Don, "I wish you to take this watch and return it whenever you choose. Am I so old I cannot send my watch to be cleaned without these busybodies rushing in? Am I so aged I cannot give my beloved daughter a machine to make some pretty clothes? I will show these lubberly cubs who is the master at Miraflores and no one shall say me nay!"

"Very well," returned Don Juan, still unruffled. "If you wish I will take the watch. And Sunday, on which day I do not work, I will bring it back, well cleaned."

"Many thanks," answered Gallardo, handing it over, "but do not leave just now. On the mesa ahead there is a race course three miles long, as smooth and level as this floor. Call back your *mozo* and tell him to start on and when you gallop you will soon overtake him. I have something important to discuss."

"Your servant, Señor!" replied Fox politely and sent his pack train away.

They sat down then in the open corredor which served as the living-room of the house and, still breathing heavily and looking wrathfully about, the old man clapped his hands for the drinks. The young maid-servant, still pop-eyed, put down the bottles and scurried away and Don Pancho poured out the wine.

"Your health, Don Juan!" he said, holding up his glass. "I drink to our better acquaintance. And I hope," he added, "you will forget my sons' insults. They are hopeless—with the manners of pure Indians."

"It is nothing," responded Fox. "I am sorry that I stopped here if it has brought on all this trouble."

"It has brought to a head what has long poisoned my happiness and caused me many sleepless nights. Do you not find as you travel about that our children have lost all gratitude—all respect for the parents they should honor?

It is so in my family—except for Elodia and my youngest son, Guillermo. He is the image of my dear father who came to Mexico in Seventy-one, the year they drove so many nobles from France. Gaillard was the name then, with many honorable titles, but he changed it in Durango to Gallardo. The people here know nothing of proud names. I have wondered," he went on, "if you are descended from that John Fox who wrote the English *Book of Martyrs.*"

"I think not," replied Don Juan politely. "More likely it was for the color of my hair."

"Ah—yes, yes!" chuckled Gallardo. "It is indeed the color of a fox. There is red hair in my family, too. You have seen it in Elodia—and my youngest son has beautiful red curls. He is the replica of my father, as handsome a French gentleman as ever came to Mexico. He had been here before, in the unfortunate campaigns of Maximilian when they tried to establish an Empire, but when he fled from France he thought it best to change his name and so I am plain Gallardo.

"In the city of Durango he met a Spanish lady of very good family and endowments. They were married and he engaged in mining. This very land here, an old Spanish grant, was purchased with the silver he mined; and in Todos Santos, the town where you are going, he developed the famous Planchas de Plata where they took out pure silver in slabs.

"On the day I was baptized so great was his joy and pride that he paved the way to the font with silver bars; but his wife, my poor mother, passed away shortly afterwards and he went out of his head with grief. Leaving the property in my name he fled to California and died; and, since that time, so badly was it managed that now it produces nothing. I hope when you reach town, since you are interested in mines, you will inspect it for yourself."

"I shall be glad to do so," answered Fox. "But now I must follow my men."

"No, no!" coaxed Gallardo, pouring him out another drink, "the sun is still high in the west. It is only that San Lázaro, this great peak above us, casts its shadow on our house. I will call my daughter and have her sing some songs—you must consider this house as your own. Do not leave me now or I shall think you are angry.—Elodia!" And she came out, smiling.

The time was soon forgotten as Don Juan sat listening, until suddenly a great darkness fell. The sun had set, but there was still wine in the bottles and supper was quickly brought on. His horse was ordered back to the stables and Gallardo took command for the evening. Scarcely was supper over and the long table cleared than he called for his German music box and, from punctured steel disks, he played many Mexican songs and in particular *La Luz de Botellas*—The Light of Bottles. For by now there was no denying that Don Francisco had gazed too long upon the light of Spanish wines and Mexican mezcal, yet his stories lost nothing from that.

Fox drank along with him glass for glass, meanwhile listening to his tales of the good old days when many a *mina antigua* turned out its mule trains of gold. It was a subject that held him close, for mining had been his business; and, seated by her father and gazing up into his eyes, Elodia, his Mariquita, smiled back at him. The light of her eyes mingled subtly with that of the *botellas* and in a strange, exalted trance he wondered at the beauty which no Mexican had been bold enough to claim.

She was a woman a little past the first glow of youth but intoxicating in her charms; a woman who, in town, would have suitors by the score, playing the bear beneath her window at night. But in isolated Miraflores she sat at her father's knee and exchanged glances with a stranger—a Yanqui! Fox drank his last glass slowly, for the old wine was going to his head, and pondered on the mystery of it all; and as he watched her she made him a sign. A mere motion of one finger before her face, but in that country it meant No. It meant: Do not.

He touched his glass inquiringly and she nodded assent. He pushed it back and she jerked her head towards the gate. Then he summoned up his strength and rose.

"Excuse me," he said to his host. "I must order my horse and go."

He clapped his hands peremptorily, shouting commands to the startled *mozo,* and shook hands with them both. His knees were a little uncertain as he paced down the flowered walk but the tang of danger had cleared his brain. There was something suspicious going on in this place—his Mariquita had signaled him to go. And the frogs which made such clamor from the swamp had suddenly stilled their croaks. A black figure glided up behind the palings of the fence, and from the darkness Elodia spoke.

"Be careful!" she said. "My brothers! They will kill you." And at a sound of running feet she was gone.

Don Juan turned and with his back to the wall stood

waiting, his head thrust out.

"Halt!" he commanded, his hand on his gun; but in the moonlight Bizco came straight on.

"Give me back that watch!" he ordered; and the American could see he was drunk. And Manuel, behind him, was drunk.

"Take yourselves away!" he rapped. "I return it only to your father."

"You come Sunday, eh?" sneered Bizco. "To make love to Elodia! Be careful, you Gringo fox. I see through you."

"And you be careful, Cock-eye, or you will find the fox a wolf."

"You will be wolf's bait if you trifle with me. You are trying to marry our sister."

"Verdad?" mocked Juan. "And is that a crime?"

"It is punished like a crime," returned Bizco. "Now give me back that watch you are trying to steal and never come here again."

"Go chase yourself," laughed Fox and at sight of his gun they turned and strode off, cursing. Then the *mozo* came hurrying with Pardo, and Don Juan rode away down the trail.

CHAPTER III

THE PICACHO PANTS

I T WAS VERY SIMPLE NOW and as Fox looked back at it he burst out laughing at the brothers. His harmless flirtation with the fair Elodia had given them the wrong idea. What? He, an American mining man, making good money selling sewing machines, to settle down and marry Mariquita? No matter if her eyes were as bright as diamonds and her tresses as fine as spun gold! No matter if she combined in her glorious figure the grace and beauty of all Mexico, he would not have her for a wife. He would marry no woman and he had a reason that brought a curse to his lips.

But flirt? He would flirt with any of them if it helped to sell a machine. Or for no reason at all—just to flirt. They tried to make a fool of him and he *made* fools of them. He had learned about women to his sorrow and now he paid them back. In their own coin, a smile for a smile, a kiss for a kiss. And when brothers—or husbands—came to warn him away he answered them with a gun on his hip.

Don Juan slapped it, a little drunkenly, and headed off down the long lane which led to the mesa beyond; but Pardo soon slowed to a walk. He was eager to go but the heavy sand held him back—it clung to his swift hoofs like invisible bands that pulled him down at each step. Then his iron-shod feet struck fire from the stones and he scrambled up the mesa. At last it opened before him, the long, level straightaway, and he started down the race track at a gallop.

The wind tugged at Fox's hat, it buffeted his face and brought water to his eyes; but Pardo had gained his head and he ran like the wind—until suddenly he rose up and came back. Juan ducked just in time to dodge a blow in the face from Pardo's bony skull and they were hurled over backwards with a smash. Yet, just in time again, he twitched one foot from the stirrup and escaped the impaling thrust of the pommel. The steel horn struck the ground, Pardo fell flat in a cloud of dust, but Fox landed on his feet. Then with a thud that shook the earth a huge giant cactus tottered and measured its length down the trail.

It had all happened too quickly for Juan to understand—the sudden check of his horse, the flailing rise of his hammer-like head, the smash as he hit the ground. But when that giant *sahuaro* was jerked down across their path he knew he had struck a rope. The next instant, out of the murk, a Mexican came rushing at him with his *machete* raised to strike. A broad cane-knife, two feet long and heavy enough to cut down a tree! Fox ducked and collided with another white-clad form. Then he jumped back and reached for his pistol.

In the blaze of his first shot he saw a low, brutal face and caught the glint of uplifted steel; but at the menacing *whang* of a gun, man and knife disappeared and the peon behind broke and ran. He plunged straight into the tangle of cacti that lined the trail like a wall and Juan's next two shots went wild. Things were coming too thick and fast and his shooting nerve was gone. He stood trembling for a moment beside the wildly snorting Pardo, then swung up into the saddle and left there. There were many good reasons for leaving and none for lingering on. His horse leapt the barrel-like trunk of the giant cactus and hit the wind for Todos Santos.

Now that he had come through it alive, Fox began to understand the cunning trap that had been set for him. The race track was a place where all horsemen proceeded at a gallop after toiling through the heavy sand and, in order to snatch him off where their knives could finish the work, the assassins had stretched a rope. But Pardo was too tall or the rope too slack and, instead of catching the rider, it had hooked his horse under the chin. A very ingenious way of putting a stranger out of the way—Juan wondered if Bizco knew about it.

He splashed through a shallow river and entered the town warily. It was at the mouth of a broad canyon that cut through the Sierras and the mountains rose straight up on three sides, but all Mexican towns are built around a square and he found the big hotel on the Plaza. A light poured forth from its *cantina* where the barkeeper was just serving the drinks and, dropping his reins on the ground, Juan stepped in and held up one finger. An American and two Mexicans set down their glasses to stare as Fox tossed off his bracer. Since he had dismounted he felt the need of a drink; and he got it, no questions asked.

"You are Señor Fox?" inquired the Spanish proprietor politely. "I am Pepe Torres, at your service. Is this your Yaqui *mozo?*"

He pointed to the corner where Fidel sat on his heels beside the heavy sack of pesos.

"*Seguro,*" replied Don Juan, putting a coin on the bar; and beckoned his faithful servant out the door.

They went in past the porter to the long courtyard behind and Fox spoke low in his ear.

"I was attacked by two Mexicans, on the mesa," he said. "They hung a rope across the trail and tried to stab me. Go back and watch the spot and follow their tracks at dawn. I want to know where they went—and who hired them."

"And then?" inquired Fidel grimly.

"Do not kill them. You will find me here."

"Very well," responded the Indian, handing over the sack of coin. "This is your room. The machines are in the warehouse."

He took Pardo's bridle and led him back to the corrals and Fox returned to the bar.

"And now, gentlemen," he said to the company, "won't you join me in a drink?"

It was not that they needed a drink—they had had plenty already—but they evidently had something on their minds.

"What's that over your eye?" asked the American bluntly. "You look like you'd been in a fight."

"Nope. Lost in the brush," returned Don Juan with a grin. "Hell of a country to travel in, after dark."

"Sure is," agreed the American. "Or any other time. I'm leaving in the morning. Going north."

Don Juan nodded and held out his hand.

"Fox is my name," he said. "John Fox."

"Glad to meet you. I'm Bozo Wilson. We were having a little game."

He jerked his thumb towards a table where three hands lay face-down, and Don Juan smiled indulgently.

"Go to it," he said, shaking hands with the two Mexicans. "I'll have a few words with the boss."

"Like to join us?" invited Wilson. "I see you're well heeled."

"Oh—this!" returned Fox, hefting the bag. "I was just

going to leave it with the proprietor."

"Lots of action for your money," insinuated Bozo. "These two *hombres* are trying to break me."

"To win them pants, eh?" jested Juan; and the Mexicans caught the joke and laughed. They called them *pantalones*.

"That's right!" swaggered Wilson, turning to give the stranger a side view. "That's just what they figger on doing. Them's the finest buckskin pants in the State of Sonora—Apolinar here is crazy about them."

He pointed to the small, wiry Mexican that Fox had spotted for a gambler and strutted proudly across the floor.

"They call 'em," he went on, "the Picacho Pants—named after Picacho de San Lázaro, this sharp mountain you see over west."

Fox looked the pants over and shook his head.

"Ump—umm!" he said, "they stand out too much behind."

"That's jest it!" declared Bozo, who was short and redheaded. "That peak is what makes 'em so good. Nice and cool, when you're riding down the trail. And soft! They're jest like a glove. Been rained on a thousand times and never shrunk an inch. Comanche-tanned—that's the answer."

Juan examined the pants again, and there was something about their cut that appealed to him. They had style, and a swagger all their own.

"Is this a selling talk?" he inquired. "All right, I'll give you twenty-five pesos for them."

"Oho!" laughed Bozo. "Don't you think it. Apolinar

has offered me a hundred."

"Sure enough?" asked Fox, and the little gambler nodded.

"I like them—there is something!" he explained in broken English. "But no! He will not sell."

"Well, *break* me first!" taunted Bozo Wilson; and Apolinar beckoned grimly.

"Very well," he said. "Be seated. How much you bet? You like to set in, my frien'?"

"Not now," answered Juan, still holding the bag of pesos. "Go ahead. Break him flat. Win his pants."

"He cain't do it!" crowed Bozo, straightening up his stacks of coin; and Fox turned away from them, laughing.

"Know those fellows?" he inquired as he leaned against the bar; and Torres answered with a nod.

"Sure," he said in Spanish. "Old friends!"

"Professionals, eh?" suggested Fox and the proprietor regarded him wisely.

"Perhaps," he admitted. "You like to play?"

"Not tonight," responded Juan, "I am tired." And he passed the sack over the bar.

A heavy silence followed, but after a long look the gamblers went ahead with their game. Fox watched them over his shoulder as he talked on with Torres and at last he edged closer and sat down.

"I'm tired," he said again; and yawned.

"There's some cards," observed Bozo, dealing him a hand with the rest; but Fox only shook his head. Then he glanced at them idly and sat up.

"You're a pretty good dealer," he remarked. "Can you

do that well for yourself?"

"And better!" grinned Wilson. "How many?"

"Gimme two," responded Fox and signaled Torres for his sack of coin.

He lost and bet higher, lost again and threw down his hand.

"Too fast for me," he said. "I'm tired."

"Try these," suggested Bozo with a wink and Juan sat up with a jerk.

"Say, you're good," he nodded. "Shall we gang these two *hombres?* Or maybe they're good, too!"

"No! Not very good!" replied Apolinar in English; and for the first time the stranger won.

"Now it's my deal!" he announced when the cards came his way. "Hold your breath. I'm an expert—back home."

He shuffled, a little awkwardly, laid the pack down for the cut and came through with a winning hand.

"Nothing like dealing your own," he observed; and the other Mexican tried his luck. A half an hour later he was out of the game and the three lucky ones played on. Bozo won, Apolinar came back at him; Fox stayed in, losing his ante every time. Then he drew the hand he was waiting for and raised them until Apolinar called him. Bozo had fallen by the wayside—all the money was on the table—and on the showdown John Fox won.

"Aha!" he said as he raked in the coin. "You'd've done better to let me go to bed."

"That is right," agreed Apolinar, regarding him thoughtfully; but Wilson was not satisfied.

"I'll play you for my pants!" he dared and Fox looked

at him over his winnings.

"And what will you wear then?" he asked.

"Never mind!" came back Bozo. "I haven't lost them yet. My pants against a hundred pesos."

"All right," answered Juan. "Or we'll draw for the high card. It's too bad about them pants."

"But I ain't lost them yet!" repeated Wilson.

"Yes you have," replied Fox as he threw down the high card. "But I'll give you another pair."

"Hell's bells!" complained Bozo. "How do you do it?"

"That's easy," laughed Don Juan. "My girl went back on me, up in the U.S.A. Since then I can't lose at cards."

"Oh! Believe in luck, eh?" grumbled Wilson. "Then you'd better not take them pants. They belonged to Bill Miller, back in Texas—he won them, riding a bronk. The very next morning he fell and broke his leg, got pneumonia and died in three days."

"I'll take a chance," shrugged Fox.

"And the feller I got them from," went on Bozo, "stole a horse and had to skip to Mexico. He got into a fight down here in Santa Maria—tried to whip all the gendarmes in town and they threw him into the hoozgar. He laid there six months until his skin turned snow white—the sun never shone down that hole. Then a girl came along and got him out, and he married her out of gratitude. They didn't have a bean in the pot when I bought these pants off of him—for five dollars."

"Say!" barked Fox, "will you please shut up and give me those *pantalones?*"

"They's a Jonah on 'em!" warned Bozo. "Don't say I didn't tell you."

"I won't!" promised Juan. "Wait till I bring you that other pair. And I'll give you five pesos, for luck."

He hurried down to his room and came back with a pair of trousers.

"Just your size!" he said, approvingly. "And here—I'll make it ten."

"Well—all right," agreed Wilson. "And say, I feel better! I feel like my luck had changed. I wondered what it was that was coppering all my bets! It was the Jonah on them pants!"

"Never mind!" grinned Fox. "I'm all man—remember that! There's no Jonah in the world that can put the curse on me. And there's something about these pants I like."

"Well, take 'em—and to hell with 'em!" yapped Bozo venomously. "I'll thank you for that ten you mentioned!"

CHAPTER IV

THE SPANISH PRISONER

FOX AWOKE AT DAWN to a sense of well-being and the smell of coffee roasting. He woke to the clangor of ancient church bells and the *shush, shush* of sandaled feet as they passed. Then his eyes fell on the glories of the Picacho Pants and his lips parted in a triumphant smile. They were his, the *pantalones* of the boastful American who had tried to break him at poker, and the joke would be all over town. He would walk forth while the girls were coming home from Mass and let them see a real man.

But there was a lump over one eye that would have to

be reduced—where he had struck the swell of the saddle as he swung quickly aside, escaping Pardo's weight by a hair. And those two white-clad peons with their cane-knives raised to strike—there was another piece of luck. And behind that—Elodia! His Mariquita with the black eyes and the clinging gown of Chinese red! What a woman! What a country! Always something exciting—and now there was a scratch on the door. The faint, secret scratch by which Fidel announced his presence, like a dog scratching fleas on the threshold.

Juan bounded out of bed, leapt into the Picacho Pants and buckled on his pearl-handled six-shooter. Then he opened the door softly and Fidel glided in, bearing a bundle wrapped up in his handkerchief. Without a word he opened it on the bed—three empty cartridges from his master's pistol, a wicked cane-knife and Gallardo's watch. Fox snatched it up and shook it anxiously—he must have dropped it in the fight, but nothing had been jarred loose. The cane-knife he knew, having seen it coming towards him in the glare of his first night shot. And he remembered the low-browed head and the eager, brutal eyes that had been behind that blow.

He nodded approval, gave the Yaqui a peso and let him out the door. Then he clapped his hands to summon a servant with hot water and made a careful toilette. After all he was there to sell sewing machines, and it is the first impression that counts. Especially with the ladies. He washed and shaved, put on a clean white shirt, and a buckskin jacket against the morning's chill; and as a last subtle touch a dab of French perfumery on his mustache. Then, the bells ringing again, he stepped out in front of the hotel to watch the black-veiled girls going by. From the church, where they had had remission of their sins and could look forward to another day.

The plaza of Todos Santos was very old, with a bandstand in the middle and a double line of paths where the boys and girls could flirt as they passed. All the girls chaperoned by sad-eyed mothers or widowed aunts, the boys laughing and making loutish jests. But now beneath the ancient palms and fat ceiba trees the maidens hurried home from their prayers. The boys were all off at their work. Don Juan was the only beau in the park and he smiled rakishly as they went by. Then he stepped into the *cantina* for his morning's dram and Pepe Torres greeted him cordially.

"My gracious!" he exclaimed in his quaint English. "You are an excellent poker player, no? Apolinar Lopez expressed the opinion that you are an adept with the cards. And Bozo—he left town at dawn."

"Couldn't stand it, eh, to see me wearing his pants? Well, Apolinar was right. I just watched to see if they were playing on the square and then I went in to win. If you've got any more gamblers that think they're professionals—"

"Bring them on, hey? But Apolinar is best. There is another one, though, that all the time goes against him. Bizco Gallardo, the son of Don Francisco, the gentleman to whom you sold the sewing machine. All the men who loaf around the low *cantinas* are in debt to Bizco from the cards, and to pay him they will do anything."

"Even cut a man's throat," suggested Fox.

"Exactly!" nodded Pepe. "I see you understand. It is all

over town that those two men try to kill you. You must be little more careful, my frien'."

"I believe you are right," agreed Don Juan, rubbing his eyebrow reflectively; and Pepe looked up the street, both ways.

"You make lof to Bizco's sister?" he asked, coming back. "Better not—plenty other girls."

"Yes, I know," answered Fox. "But why not? I'm a stranger here—I don't understand."

"No! No!" replied Torres, a wealth of meaning in his smile. "You're a new man—you don' onderstand."

He looked out the door, glanced quickly into the patio and beckoned Juan up close.

"You notice the pesos you bring in last night? Been buried, eh? Smell like dirt. Don Francisco has *muchos! Muchos!* And the man that marries Elodia gets all!"

"The hell!" exclaimed Fox. "But I don't want to marry her."

"Makes no difference!" stated Pepe. "You flirt with her, no? Then Bizco runs you out of the country!"

"Runs *me* out!" repeated Don Juan incredulously.

"Or he keels you!" added Torres. "For six years now Elodia tries to get married. No use—he runs them all off."

"Why, the rascal!" laughed Fox. "What does he want to do that for?"

"What for!" repeated Pepe. "So she don' have a hosband, to protect her. If she ain't got a man she is not *casada*. She is nothing—only a woman!"

"Oh, I see," nodded Fox, although he did not. "Well, too bad, but she can't have me. I wouldn't marry the richest woman in the country. Much obliged, Don Pepe, for spelling it all out to me. We Americans are kind of *tonto,* no?"

"Well—sometimes," admitted Torres, regretfully. "You going back to see that girl?"

"Quien sabe," shrugged Juan with a grin. "Say, you're a Spaniard, eh? Ever heard that old joke about Kin Savvy? An American saw a funeral going by and asked a Mexican whose it was.

" *'Quien sabe,'* he says, and the Yanqui slaps his leg.

" 'Well, I'm glad that so-and-so is dead,' he says. 'Now if this old geezer *Mañana* would just pass away we might get something done in this country.' "

"Yes! Ha, ha!" laughed Torres. "Very good—very good! But one word—come here just a moment. A man leaves word with me to give you a message, not to go to Miraflores next Sunday. Better not, eh? I will send back the watch."

"Oh, the watch!" said Fox. "Say, you people know everything. Was this man that left the message cock-eyed?"

"Cock-eyed? I don' quite onderstand!"

"Was his first name Bizco—that's all I want to know. Well, tell him I'll be there, with bells."

The church bells were ringing on Sunday morning as Don Juan rode back up the trail, his second pistol in his belt. Also his rifle was on the saddle and Fidel carried his old repeater. After so many warnings from Pepe Torres, Fox had decided to travel heeled. Not that Bizco was so much, but just to be prepared—and there might be Yaquis on the trail. Bronco Yaquis, waiting to give some

Gringo a birthday party and strip him as naked as he was born. Fidel might talk them out of killing him, but Fox was wearing his Picacho Pants.

The old French watch that Gallardo valued so highly was ticking gently under Don Juan's fancy sash and, with a couple of drinks to bring his courage up to par, he was all set for a frolic or a fight. There would be wine, he knew that, and golden mezcal, and the music box to play *La Luz de Botellas*—and perhaps, who could tell, a kiss from Mariquita, for now he knew her secret. He understood at last why she was so loving and so free. All the Mexican boys were afraid to come and see her and she was afraid she would die an old maid.

"Adalante!" he cried when they came to the race track; but Fidel held up his hand. Then he rode on ahead, looking both ways for an ambush, and Fox let him go. He came from a warlike people who rather specialized in ambushes and were equally keen in detecting them, and the sight of his grim face and the repeating cannon across his lap might deter even Bizco's low felons. Fox had heard more than a little about this squint-eyed son of perdition and if only half the stories were true he had a tough band of cutthroats at his back. Men who knew every trick of the old Spanish *ladrones,* men who made man-killing a business. So they took the long straight-away at a wary trot and came safely to the sandy lane.

It was a surprise, perhaps, to Bizco and Manuel to see the American riding down the slope and they showed themselves in the open; but Juan took the lead and came straight on, with one pistol tucked under his knee. That made it very handy in case of a surprise, and who would be looking for one there? Not Bizco, not Manuel—and, as Fox had his Yaqui behind him, they held up their hands for a talk.

"We have come," began Bizco, "to demand our father's watch. After that it will not be necessary to go further."

"After what?" demanded Fox. "Do you think I would trust you with his watch? No, Señores, I have learned your reputation—you might steal it, as you have other things from him."

At this the handsome face of Bizco turned red and then changed to the pale fixedness of hate, but he did not draw his gun.

"Ha, assassin!" he cried angrily, "we know the purpose of this insult and refuse to be drawn into your trap. I saw you put the pistol under your leg. We knew you had come to kill us."

"Not unless you try to kill me," answered Fox; and they wheeled and galloped away. Up the lane and in past the house, and Don Juan followed close behind them. The whole family was gathered in the corredor, Elodia in a gorgeous new dress, and Fox waved at her gallantly as he brought his horse to a stop and left him for the Yaqui to watch. Then, still wearing his two pistols, he strode up to the porch and saluted them with his high-peaked sombrero.

"Good morning, Don Francisco!" he hailed. "I have brought you back your watch. And since I am not very welcome I will put it in your hands and go."

"No, no!" replied Gallardo. "You are very welcome indeed. Please enter—my poor house is yours."

"I should like to," answered Fox with a glance at his Mariquita, "but your sons have met me down the road and told me not to stay. So, rather than have to kill them, I will go."

He held out the watch but, when the old man saw it running, he clasped him to his breast.

"Ah, my friend!" he cried. "Have you made it run again? And my two ungrateful sons would have it no other way but that you would never bring it back."

"No," assented Juan. "They sent me a message not to come. But you put this watch in my hand and I swore I would put it in yours. Good-by, my good friend! *Adios, Señoras!*" And he turned with a flourish to leave.

"But Señor Fox!" called Gallardo. "I have not paid you for mending it! This old watch that I value so much!"

"It is nothing!" replied Don Juan. "A small thing for an old friend. No, Señor! Not a centavo! I must go!"

"But no!" protested the old man. "I have important business to discuss. And Elodia has made a new dress."

He waved his hand toward Mariquita, who spread out her skirt coquettishly, and Don Juan looked and fell. It was a gorgeous gown, made of brocaded red silk, and the black spots were like the markings of a ladybird. He glanced down toward the corrals, where Bizco and Manuel were watching him, and strode gallantly back to admire.

"The dress is beautiful!" he said. "But not half as charming as the transcendent lady who wears it. Were it not that her brothers have forbidden me to see her—"

"They are nothing! I have disowned them!" roared Gallardo. And shook his fist towards the corrals.

"And have I your permission," inquired Fox, with an exaggerated bow, "to remain and call on your daughter? And you, Señora? Your permission?"

"You have, sir!" replied Doña Luz; and her husband took Don Juan by the hand.

"Elodia," he said, "I present my good friend, Don Juan Fox; a man of honor, as we know. And after we have discussed the matter of my mine I shall ask you to entertain him."

"Your servant, Papá," responded Mariquita demurely; and gave Juan a last look as she retired. It caused him to forget that her brothers had promised to kill him if he ever made love to her again. It made him dizzy, like wine, before with Old World courtesy her father poured out the first drink. Then the syncope passed and he found himself listening to a long dissertation on the mine. The Planchas de Plata, where they had once taken out slabs of silver, but which was now given over to the bats.

"And have you examined it?" he demanded anxiously. "I have been waiting to hear your opinion."

"No, Señor," replied Fox, "I have not. I have no wish, as you know, to have trouble with your sons; and so I have stayed away. But from the plaza the formation looks very good and I hear there are *gambusinos* at work."

"Ore thieves! In my mine? I must look into this! But have no fear of my sons. Manuel is a good boy, but weak; and Bizco I have disowned. He stays here, for his mother still loves him; but legally he is no longer my son. I find that he has deceived me in order to get my gold."

"Nevertheless," said Juan, "I cannot examine your

mine; and in a few days I am going south. Even to look at the Planchas de Plata might seem presumptuous and I do not wish to kill your son."

"He may as well be killed," stormed Gallardo, "as remain to disgrace my name. You have heard in Todos Santos how he consorts with the lowest peons, drinking and gambling and wasting his money? That I could bring myself to forgive. But he has robbed his own father and made me a laughing-stock—have you ever heard of the Spanish Prisoner Swindle?"

"Yes, indeed," nodded Fox. "It is an old one."

"And how, then, does it go?"

"Why, an old man writes from Madrid that he is in prison, and he has a great treasure buried somewhere that he wishes to give you before he dies."

"Yes, yes!" exclaimed Don Francisco in great vexation. "And what does he want of you?"

"Only," explained Juan, "that you come to Spain and release him, so he can give you a map of the spot."

"And is that all?" demanded Gallardo.

"Well," grinned Fox, "there's generally a mortgage on his castle or a big fine to pay—"

"And he asks you to bring him ten thousand dollars!"

"That's the idea," admitted Juan. "Did you get one?"

"No!" cried Gallardo. "It came to my son—and he knew it was a swindle, all the time. But in order to steal my savings he pretended to believe it and at last I was convinced. Then he got me to give him ten thousand dollars in gold to get this poor man out of jail. He took the money to Madrid and spent it in the dance halls. And this is how I know! Read that!"

He slammed down a printed circular from the Spanish Government, warning strangers against the swindle, and Don Juan nodded his head.

"Yes. That is it," he said.

"You knew it, all the time, eh? Well, so did Bizco! But he pretended to be taken in. He made a fool of his own father in order to get my gold, and now I have the proof. Only for his mother I would have him arrested—I would kill him with my own hand. Ah, you scoundrel—you low-lived profligate!" he shouted, suddenly shaking his fist again. "I have found you out! Begone! You have robbed your poor father, but you shall not linger on to ruin your sister's life! This *caballero* has come to court her—now fight him, if you dare. But beware, or he will kill you!"

He stood glaring as his two sons wheeled their horses and spurred away up the slope of the mesa. Then he turned to Don Juan with a smile.

"Would you like, now," he said, "a few words with Elodia?"

Fox nodded. There was no answer but Yes.

CHAPTER V

AN OLD MAID

THERE WAS SOME MISTAKE in this strange turn of the wheel of Fate, but Don Juan had no time to search it out. Elodia came forth smiling, her eyes so radiant with love that he felt himself a conqueror—a very hero. He had touched the Sleeping Beauty and brought her back to life again; he had released the Fairy Princess from the sway of her cruel brothers, who had denied her to all suitors; he had restored to her her woman's right to seek out the man she loved. But she had bestowed that honor upon him, and Fox had other plans.

That day in Todos Santos a grand fiesta was on, with horse races and chicken-pulls and pistol shooting, and he had promised Pepe Torres to return. They had a plan to trim the local sports by a frame-up in the shooting contests, but now Mariquita held his thoughts. She was thanking him for driving the false Bizco away—and what a glory there was in her eyes! Yet as he looked back to the morning he could find no intent to play the bear.

As he remembered, he had come to Miraflores solely to deliver Gallardo his watch; but in some way he had become committed to play the lover to poor Elodia when in reality he wished nothing of the kind. It was just that, in his defiance of the sinister Bizco, he had gone a little too far. But there was ardor in her touch, adoration in her eyes and, without concerning himself too much about the future, he played a leading hand.

"Shall we walk in the garden?" he inquired gallantly; and the old man gave his consent. All the traditions of cloistered Old Mexico were swept away for his sake and he found himself alone with Mariquita. They touched hands again as he helped her down the steps and he felt his resolution fail. Always before in his Mexican love affairs there had been an iron grille, to protect the girl—and him. They spoke in the language of flowers and dropped handkerchiefs, of languishing glances and kisses stolen through the bars; but in the dark room behind there was always the muffled duenna, ready to appear when his daring went too far. Then the romantic approach became a strategic retreat and he passed blithely on to the next town. All was changed now—but there was still the next town.

Mariquita glanced at him roguishly and let her handkerchief fall, he picked it up and plucked a red rose for her hair; then they strolled on, smiling at nothing, and in the splendor of garden and sky they beheld a new heaven, a new earth. There was a rainbow, an aureole, that hung above the palms, painting their paradise in magic hues; and in every tufted tree a cooing white-winged dove seemed expiring in a delirium of love. Juan felt the spell of her presence, the bewitching madness which swayed all Nature, and took her hand in his own.

"Did you see me?" she asked at last, "when you came to the brow of the mesa and I looked up from the house? I was told you would come from the north."

"Yes?" he murmured, politely. "And by whom?"

"By a Gypsy—a fortune teller—who came here with her husband. She told me you would come.

"'Not tall,' she said. 'Not short. Not broad—not narrow. Not fat—not thin. An American—with red hair.'"

"That's me," admitted Fox and sought to turn the conversation, for Gypsies always told about husbands.

"And she said," went on Elodia, smiling dreamily, "I should know you by that color. It is the color of my embodiment—red! Do you remember the red silk handkerchief you wore? I wondered if some fortune teller had read *your* hand and told you your destiny was here."

"Not me!" he answered, releasing her hand. "I don't believe in that stuff. Just cross their palms with two dollars instead of one and they'll make it twice as good. Or cut them down to a *real* and all they can see is hard work, lots of children and trouble."

She laughed and pushed him away.

"And is that so bad?" she inquired. "Think of the curse that Bizco had laid upon me. Never to marry! To die an old maid! For six years I waited and saw my beauty fade, and no man came to defend me. They came—yes! To make love! But when Bizco spoke they went away. Do you wonder that I watched the trail? 'An American!' she said. 'Not tall—not short. He will drive your brother away!'"

"Away?" repeated Fox, looking up.

"Yes, indeed!" she answered, and there was iron in her voice. "Out of the country! Never to come back!"

"Well, well!" observed Juan. "That is quite a contract. Will your father and mother consent?"

"Oh, yes!" she said. "They have!"

"And suppose," he suggested, "I should have to kill Bizco?"

"You will not!" she said positively. "The Gypsy so stated. Is my Redhead, then, afraid?"

"Not of him," replied Fox, pacing on down the path. "But what would your father say?"

"It is best," she said, naively, "that Bizco should go. Everything that he does is evil. Did he not try to have you murdered—on the mesa?"

"Yes—but why?" demanded Don Juan.

"Why, to keep you from marrying me!"

"Oh!" said Fox, and his voice turned hard. "Did I say I would marry you? No—I said the other way! I would not marry the best woman in the world!"

"No?" cried Elodia, starting back; and into her dark eyes there came the black shadow of despair. "Will nobody have me, then?" she wailed. "Must I become an old maid and have all the people laugh at me? The Gypsy woman said you would come!"

"Pah! Horse doctors! Chicken thieves!" spat Juan contemptuously. "What do these Gypsies know about the future? You are a fine girl—I like you—but not that much. Marry some Mexican, when I am gone."

"Santa Maria!" she sighed, sinking down on a stone bench and blinking back the tears. "Have I been fooled by these accursed Gitanos? You do not love me? You did not come to save me?"

"No," he said. "I came to sell sewing machines. And soon I am going away."

"*Madre de Dios!* Then do not tell my father and mother. They think you are crazy to marry me. And when you go will you do me a favor? Give me a kiss, then. Hold my hand. Make love the way they expect."

"To be sure!" answered Don Juan, laughing. "And what will you give me for that?"

"My love! My whole self! Anything! Only drive Bizco out of the country!"

"With pleasure!" he said. "But let us practice that kiss!" And he rose up and swept her into his arms. They kissed rapturously, kissed again, and she thrust him away.

47

"Oh, I love you!" she sighed. "I love you."

"No use!" he answered roughly. "I am a Yanqui—understand? I kiss all of them and marry none."

"Ah, my Redhead—my sweetheart!" she murmured. "Are all men, then, the same?"

"They are!" he said. "And all women! I trusted one, to my sorrow. I'll never trust another again."

"But Juanito!" she coaxed, laying her cheek against his; and he kissed her before he put her away.

"You love me, eh?" he grinned. "Very well, I will drive him away."

"And then?" she asked expectantly.

"I will go," he said, "and never come back."

"And must I be an old maid? All my life!"

"No!" he barked. "Marry a Mexican! Isn't the country full of them?"

"But I love you," she pleaded. "Best."

"Nope—nope," he said. "You're trying to jolly me. It's time I took you back to your father. Then I'm going to Todos Santos to hunt up your fine brother and run him out of the country."

CHAPTER VI

SEÑOR SNAKE-EYES

THE LEAVE-TAKING of Don Juan from his Mariquita was all that a lady could expect. He kissed her hand, he whispered in her ear and stole a little kiss as he fled; but Elodia knew him now and she gazed after him sadly. It was true then—they were all the same.

Fox rode into the crowded plaza of Todos Santos with a single purpose in mind—to seek out Bizco Gallardo wherever he might be and give him the scare of his life. To run him out of the country as he had chased his sister's suitors, and make his name a byword and a hissing. But when he came to the Gran Hotel de España, Pepe Torres beckoned him in and looked him over expectantly.

"Well," he said in his very good English, "do we shake down these small-town es-sports?"

"Seguro que sí!" laughed Juan. "I had forgotten all about it!"

"Then you must have some trouble with Bizco—eh, my frien'? He just came to town, with Manuel."

"Well—perhaps," shrugged Fox. "But mostly the trouble was his. Don Francisco has received a letter from the Spanish Government and he has disowned them. Sent them away."

"Ah! That Spanish Prisoner Swindle! The poor father was the last to believe. But we in town have known for a year that Bizco did it of a purpose. He has bad blood, that boy—a little *siniestro*—over the left. A brother of his mother was executed by the Rurales. A *bandido,* though nothing is said of it."

"I—see!" nodded Juan. "Is Bizco bad, then?"

"With his gang behind him—yes! You must be careful, my frien'! But I will be there to protect you."

"And Fidel," added Fox, with a glance at his body-guard. "Come on, then. I will show you some shooting."

"But not at first!" warned Pepe. "We must get them to bet. *Empalmar cinco tiros*—to place five shots within the space of a hand—that is their favorite sport. Can you do that, of a certainty, my frien'?"

"At thirty yards—and my horse at a gallop. Or put a playing card on a tree and I will shoot out every pip."

"I will take a hundred pesos more," decided Torres; and they rode down to where the guns were popping.

The shooting grounds for the fiesta were down by a wash that ran along the side of the ridge, but no one was palming five shots. Five roosters had been buried in the sand and their heads were the targets for the pistols.

"Tira los!" went up the cry from the crowd that had gathered and a curly-headed boy on a blooded black charged galloping down the course. Out came his pistol, he fired fast as he spurred by, and two heads lopped over and lay still.

"That is Yermo, the brother of Bizco," confided Pepe. "Shall we lose a few pesos to him?"

"Sure!" agreed Fox. "But say, where does he live? I never see him at home."

"With his oncle, Nicolás. He cannot bear his two brothers. *Oye, Yermo!* My frien', Señor Fox."

"Su servidor!" greeted Guillermo. "Will you shoot at the roosters? I am betting five pesos I win."

"With pleasure," replied Juan. "This is a new kind of target."

"But very good—we can eat the roosters. See, my *mozo* has eight already. The charge is a peso a course."

The man who conducted the shoot had hurried to bury two more roosters and now he delivered the dead ones to Yermo.

"Another round?" he demanded eagerly.

"This gentleman will shoot first," bowed the boy. "You are a friend of my father, no?"

"Yes—I sold him a sewing machine," grinned Juan. "But clear the way, now. I am going to shoot."

He rode Pardo down the course and drew his pistol once for practice. Then, back at the start, he spurred forward at a gallop and fired five times at the heads. They dodged, the sand flew, but not a comb was scratched, and young Yermo dashed out with a whoop. One, two— the heads flew off—and he came back without shooting more.

"I have killed ten now," he said. "We are riding too close. I will match you for ten pesos this time and give you two heads start."

"No, Señor!" protested Fox. "I am as good a shot as you are. It is only that I have not caught the knack."

He charged down the course and killed two birds out of the five, but Yermo won with three.

"You are learning," he said. "I will shoot with you again."

"For twenty pesos!" challenged Juan and a crowd gathered to watch the contest. They were shooting fast and furiously when a band of horsemen rode out from town and in the lead Juan saw Bizco, laughing.

"Aha, Gringo!" he jeered. "You talk big, but even a boy can beat you. Now shoot a round with a man!"

"You mean yourself?" inquired Fox. "Who are all this gang at your back?"

"My friends!" announced Bizco, meaningly.

"*Carai!*" spoke up Yermo insultingly. "What a lot of bums they are. Shoot with me, Señor Snake-eyes—

I can beat you."

"Shut your mouth!" retorted Bizco. "I am talking to this Gringo who wears Bozo Wilson's pants—but that does not make him a man. Shoot with me, I say, and make good your boasts or I will run you out of the country."

"Shoot for fun or for money? You who talk so loud—I will bet a hundred pesos I can beat you."

"I will bet you two hundred!" came back Bizco. "This is like picking up money in the streets."

"Put it up, then," answered Fox signaling Torres. "Here is my money sack—I will bet it all."

"And I," announced Yermo, "I will bet this much more."

"Have we money?" inquired Bizco, turning to his shamefaced friends. "Then, Pancho, ride back to the *cantina* and ask Esteban to bring five hundred pesos."

"We will cover it all," promised Pepe Torres. "But who will hold the stakes?"

"Apolinar Lopez!" suggested Juan as he saw the little gambler in the crowd; and reluctantly Bizco agreed.

"But he is no friend of mine," he stated, "and I warn him not to try any trickery. If I shoot off the most heads I want the money in my hands—and a bloody comb counts for a hit."

"Very well," agreed Apolinar. "But I am the judge. Do not try to dispute my decision."

"Here comes Esteban," cheered the crowd and a burly man rode up sweating, weighed down by two sacks of pesos. One glance at his face and Don Juan knew him—it was the low-browed *cholo* who had leapt out of the night to strike him down with his machete. But the money was being counted, it was no time to pick a quarrel, and he went back to the start with his enemy.

"After you," he said politely and Bizco skinned his even white teeth.

"Many thanks, Señor Yanqui," he answered. "When I have won your money we will talk of something else. I have endured your presence long enough."

"Very well," replied Fox. "Now show me how to shoot."

"Viva!" yelled the crowd as Bizco spurred his horse out and drew his pistol with a flourish; but when he rode past the roosters, buried deep in the sand, he shot off only three heads.

"This other one is blooded," he declared, riding back.

"No, sir! It is not!" denied Torres.

"I say yes!" retorted Bizco, dropping down and feeling its head; and on the comb there appeared a drop of blood. "You put that there yourself!" charged Apolinar, fiercely. "There is no bullet hole—not a break in the skin."

"No difference," came back Bizco. "You know our agreement. Did I not show you the drop of blood?"

"Yes, and there is where you got it—from that other rooster's head. You cannot play tricks on me. I know you, Crooked-eyes—your score is only three."

"It is four!" declared Bizco heatedly.

"Well, stand out of the way!" shouted Juan impatiently. "Clear the track and let a *man* try. If I cannot beat his four I will pay the bets myself. No one can call *me* a cheap sport!"

"Do you call me one, then?" bristled Bizco. "I have endured enough from you, Gringo. You would do better to stick to your sewing machines—teaching women to sew ruffles on their underwear."

A loud guffaw went up from the crowd and Fox felt his cheeks burn with shame, but he wheeled and rode to the start. Then he turned and galloped back and as he passed the buried roosters he fired evenly, timing each shot. And each time, just as evenly, a head fell in the sand until all five of them lay in a row. The secret was out—he had been stalling with young Yermo, and Bizco had lost his bet. He sat gaping as Juan loped back for his money and Apolinar held up his hand.

"The Yanqui wins!" he announced with a grin. "Here, Pepe, is the sack."

"Ha, ha!" laughed Fox, filling his empty gun with cartridges and facing Bizco the while. "How is that for a sewing machine agent?"

"You cheated!" accused Bizco in a fury. "You let Yermo beat you on purpose. I say the money is mine!"

"And I say," came back Fox, "you will never get it while I can fan a gun. You and your gang of toughs! Draw your pistol and I will kill you! And my Yaqui will take care of your gang!"

"Yes, and count me in, *cuñado*," spoke up Yermo. "I have been practising up to fight Señor Snake-eyes."

There was a delicate compliment in thus calling him *cuñado*, or brother-in-law, for it meant he was welcome to court his sister, but the word did not set well with Bizco. He glanced back and, as if at a signal, Esteban spurred up beside him.

"Gringo!" began Bizco, "you have been here long enough, making trouble between me and my people. Now I warn you to leave town by sunset or something worse will befall you."

Juan looked back at Fidel—at Yermo, Pepe and Apolinar—and advanced his horse a step.

"You would murder me, eh?" he said. "But that is not so easy. And here is one I know is an assassin!"

He fixed his eyes on Esteban and, jumping Pardo straight at him, he struck him to the ground with his six-shooter.

"Now, Cock-eye!" he challenged. "Your hired killer is down. I tell *you* to leave this town or I will kill you."

"Yes! And I tell you the same!" joined in Yermo.

Bizco glanced from one to the other and at the black Yaqui behind them and his evil eyes became infinitely sly.

"I will go," he said. "That is better than walking into a trap. But some day I will come back."

He reined his horse away and, with Esteban behind him, rode slowly into town. That evening, with Manuel, he took the trail to Chihuahua. The next day Fox started south.

CHAPTER VII

THE BITE OF A *MATAVENADO*

TWO MONTHS PASSED and the rainy season had begun before Fox came back up the trail. All the money he had received from the sale of his sewing machines was hidden in the bottoms of four pack boxes, and all he had won at poker. It made quite a load; and, as his winnings were known, he rode with a gun across the saddle. Fidel followed behind with a wary eye for ambush and neither spoke a word.

Having traveled mostly at night to escape highway robbers, Don Juan had let his beard grow, and there was no more perfumery on his mustache. All that foolishness had passed—he was a mining man now—and any Mexican who mentioned sewing machines was liable to get a crack in the jaw. He had an eye out for *minas antiguas,* the old workings of the Spaniards, but the pretty girls he passed by.

As he turned into the plaza of Todos Santos he glanced up at the red hill to the east, where the Planchas de Plata lay. Like all true *minas antiguas* it was toward the rising sun from its town and visible from the door of the church; and now, if Gallardo was still willing, Fox had money to work it. That is, if he could get an option and the *gambusinos* would allow him to operate. For if they, working secretly and at night, could gopher out enough ore to make wages he could make the old mine pay big.

His imagination was afire with dreams of wealth and grandeur, and in his thoughts the old plaza was astir with new life where now hardly a human stirred. Only hawkers selling candy and fruit; only dogs and burros, asleep in the sun; but as he turned into the courtyard of the Gran Hotel de España he stopped short and his heart missed a beat. A row of black-clad women sat crouched against the wall, their eyes on a certain door, and their lips were moving in prayer.

"What is the matter? Who is sick?" he demanded as

Pepe Torres came out. His rotund face was covered with sweat, his cheeks haggard, his eyes set; and he hardly knew his old friend.

"It is Marcelina," he said. "My little girl—she is dying. I go now to make the coffin."

"Yes, but what is the matter?" cried Juan. "I am a *curandero,* a doctor—"

"It makes no difference, my friend. She has been bitten by a *matavenado.*"

"My God!" exclaimed Fox, leaping down from his horse and fumbling for his medicine kit. The "deer-killer" was a small, hairy bug whose bite was almost always fatal; but for just such cases he had permanganate of potassium, all dissolved and ready to inject.

"Let me in!" he begged. "I can save her, perhaps. Has the *medico* given her up?"

"He has come and gone. There is nothing to do. When the *matavenado* bites one there is nothing but to make the coffin."

He passed on towards the storeroom, but as Fox stood hesitating a little woman darted out the door. It was Maria, Torres' wife, but now Juan hardly knew her. Of all the women in Todos Santos her madonna-like face had seemed the sweetest, the most radiant with motherly love, but now it was disfigured with grief.

"Come in!" she said quickly. "The doctor did nothing, but perhaps your medicine can cure her. My poor little one—my only child, except the baby! And now the *matavenado* has killed her!"

"Not yet!" answered Fox as he made his way through the crowd of weeping women. "Make room—I believe I can save her."

He fought his way to the bedside and drew back. Many times during his stay there he had held Marcelina on his knee and admired her childish beauty; but now it had vanished, destroyed. Her face, racked and twisted with fierce convulsions, was turning a mottled black and her breath came in choking gasps.

"Bring a bottle of mezcal," he said to Maria. "And then a lot of onions, newly crushed. I will try—but these women must go."

He waved them out the door, opened his kit on the table and injected permanganate into the bite. Then he bent over anxiously, feeling the faint beat of the heart, noting the labored, whistling breath—and he saw he was a little late. Too late, perhaps, for she had been bitten three hours before and the poison was closing her throat. But her heart! He wet a piece of cotton with the fiery mezcal and squeezed it, drop by drop, between her teeth.

"Now turpentine!" he ordered and rubbed it over her chest to break the clutch of death. Then more mezcal, to keep her alive until Maria came running with the onions. This was country-doctor medicine—he bound a heavy poultice about her throat and the pungent fumes made the child gasp; but after a struggle she caught her breath and relaxed.

"She is dead!" cried the mother, leaning closer; but Fox could feel her heart beat on.

"No," he said, "I may cure her yet if the venom has not gone too far. Now tell all these women to go away and keep still—our little one must have the air."

The crowd moved away and into the fetid room a

breath of outside air found its way, but as Marcelina struggled for her life a heavy pounding came from next door. It was her father, making a coffin for the funeral which so soon must follow her death.

"Tell Pepe," said Fox, "that his hammering disturbs her. There is hope—I cured a man at Santa Anita."

Maria ran out quickly, the pounding ceased, and soon she was back beside him.

"Don Juan," she said, "my child is the same as dead. Her little heart is almost still. If you cure her she is yours."

"*Madre de Dios!*" groaned Pepe, coming in. "Is my baby still alive? Then if you save her she is yours—I say so, too. For now she is the same as dead."

"Many thanks, Don Pepe," answered Fox. "I do not wish to take her from her parents. It is for you, my friend—and for Maria, her mother—that I am using my poor skill. But stop making the coffin and send the people away. When the time comes I will call you back."

He hung over the child alone, trying to force her teeth apart and open up the constricted throat, and when she took a natural breath he gave her a drink and a tablet of digitalis. Then gradually the weakened heart resumed its normal beat and he beckoned the parents in. They stood over her enraptured, scarcely believing the change which the simple remedies had produced; and Maria threw her arms around Juan.

"She is yours!" she cried. "But for you she would be dead." And Torres gave him a tearful *embrazo*.

"My friend," he sobbed, "the saints sent you to save her. Everything that I have is yours."

The drinks were free that night at Pepe's *cantina* and, when Fox came out for his, he shook hands with many men who had hurried to witness the miracle. There were hard-handed wood-choppers and dignified *hacendados,* together with the people of the town; and after each introduction Torres repeated the same formula.

"Anything you can do for Señor Fox is the same as if you do it for me."

Juan thanked them all and went back to his patient, feeling that all Todos Santos was his friend. He sat far into the night, watching over Marcelina until she fell into an easy sleep, but he could not regard her as his child. What to Maria had seemed so magical was just the skill of the country doctor provided with a medical kit. A simple cure, but it had saved her life.

So in one way she was his—and after a little time he could become her *padrino,* her godfather. He could give her foolish presents and hold her on his knee; but she still belonged to happy, smiling Pepe and Maria, the mother who had borne her. That was best—and when he went away he could leave her a dowry, for her wedding when she was grown. But now he would accept her and say she was his daughter and make much of her while he worked his mine. It would make her parents happy to think they had paid him with that which was dearest to them.

Morning came, and while he lingered over his patient a shadow fell across the barred window. It was a woman, peering in to see if Marcelina was alive; and soon another came. Then the first unwrapped a baby from her shawl and held it up to him, hopefully.

"No, no," he said, shaking his head. "I am sorry—you

must take him to your doctor. It is against the law for me to practise medicine."

He waved her away, but another shadow took her place. They came in a procession—the sick, halt and blind—even the beggars whose infirmities were their livelihood; and though he refused them all they still lingered on, dimly hoping for another miracle. But the *medico* was there, too, his eyes hot with hate, and Don Juan sent the sick ones away. Only for one thing would he try his skill—the bite of the *matavenado*.

Yet his fame had traveled far and for the next three days people came to gaze at him. When Marcelina could leave her bed, her bandaged leg smelling rank of iodoform, and sit smiling in his lap, there was a rush of people to see; and among them, his blue eyes twinkling, came Yermo, Gallardo's son.

"Que hay, Amigo," he hailed. "What is doing? You are a doctor now!"

"So it appears," replied Juan, a little grimly. "How is your father? And all the family?"

"They are well," answered Yermo. "And when your patient improves he sends word he would like to see you."

"Many thanks," returned Fox. "I had intended to come before but my little daughter would not permit it. Yet tomorrow, I think, she will let me go. Eh, Chiquita?" And he held her close.

"There is one in Miraflores," observed Yermo oracularly, "who will be jealous if you stay away too long."

"Then tell her," responded Don Juan, "that I will come in the morning. Very early! To kiss her hand!"

CHAPTER VIII

NUMBER ONE!

VERY EARLY, as he had promised, while maidens still paced up from the river with water jars balanced on their heads, Don Juan took the trail to Miraflores. In the clean-washed sultry air there was the smell of greasewood and tropical flowers in bloom and on every fluted column of giant cactus the ripe fruit made a purple crown. The double peak of San Lázaro rose sheer above the clouds that were gathering for the daily rain and the sun was smiting hot, but Fox took the race course at a gallop.

There was something mysterious about this summons to Miraflores; something portentous, either good or bad. He wondered if it had anything to do with Elodia and with his kissing her beneath the palms. And then their farewell, that sad piece of play-acting with the censorious Doña Luz looking on. Mexican mothers could never understand. They were prone to leap to unjustified conclusions, founded doubtless on their own past experience, but all the more difficult to laugh off. And Elodia—what would he say to her?

It had been hard, at their last meeting, to tell Mariquita that the Gypsy fortune teller was wrong. And yet sometimes the rascals were right. But who would have thought, seeing her watching the north trail, that she was expecting her Prince Charming to appear? The red-headed American, neither tall nor short, who came to save her from being an old maid.

He galloped across the mesa where Esteban had way-laid him and from the brow of the hill looked down on Miraflores, gleaming white among the trees and palms. It was a sobering thought that he was going to meet her, this woman who loved him too well—this woman whose eyes held a dark glow of passion, whose lips had pulsed against his.

To set her free he had chased away Bizco and weak-faced, swaggering Manuel. He had kissed her before her parents, but she knew the answer. Not for the prettiest woman in the world! There was no way out now but straight ahead—he gave Pardo his head and they clat-tered down the slope, crossed the river bottom and trotted up to the gate.

Elodia was there—their eyes met across the distance and her face lit up with a smile—but the color of her embodiment was gone. Now the red of the ladybird had given place to somber black and her mother stood up straight and forbidding. There were bows, formal greet-ings, and the ladies retired. Gallardo beckoned his guest to a chair.

"My friend," he said, after the small talk was over, "with your permission I wish to ask you a question."

"You have it," answered Fox.

"My wife wants to know," stated the old man, "if you are a suitor for my daughter's hand."

"No, sir, I am not," replied Don Juan. "I will never marry any woman."

"Perhaps," suggested Gallardo after a silence, "you have a wife in the United States?"

"No!" came back Fox, his voice rising; and Gallardo glanced towards the half-door.

"That is all," he said with a friendly smile. "I believe I understand. You were threatened by Bizco and Manuel, and to spite them you made love to Elodia."

"Perhaps," admitted Juan; and he too glanced towards the door. "Your daughter is very beautiful," he added. "I am sorry if I went too far."

"If you did," replied Don Francisco, suddenly finding his voice, "you made up for it by driving them away. My evil sons have gone to Chihuahua, to join others of their kind, and we can now live our lives in peace."

He sighed and at a clap of the hands the pop-eyed maid brought out the wine.

"Your health!" said Gallardo. "And now let us talk business. At last I am master in my house. I can carry on my work without interference and I am going to open up my mine."

"That is good," answered Fox, and waited. He had hoped for something like this.

"They have gone," went on the old man, "to join the *revoltosos* in their uprising against that great man, Porfirio Diaz. But his Rurales and soldiers will soon put it down, as they have many others before. This Cruz Pizano who is stealing cattle and robbing the mines is a *bandido,* a low *pelado*—not a patriot who loves his country. And the men who have joined him are runaway peons and wastrels like my own two sons. But I have disowned them—they are my sons no longer. Have you been up to examine my mine?"

His eyes lit up eagerly but Juan shook his head.

"Not yet. Have I your permission?"

"Why, yes! Of course! You are a strange man, Señor Fox. Does not everybody go up there? Or perhaps you are no longer interested?"

"Oh, yes!" replied Fox. "I have sold all my sewing machines and am trying to buy a good mine."

"Indeed!" beamed Don Francisco. "Then you are trained in that business! How much will you charge me to examine my property and perhaps open up the mine?"

"For you, Don Pancho, I will examine it for nothing and give you an estimate of the cost. I have worked in other mines—in Arizona and New Mexico—and know ore deposits, assaying and mill work. Have you ever thought of selling the Planchas? I have a little money saved up."

"How much?" inquired Gallardo, politely.

"Well—around eight thousand pesos. It is not very much but this is what I will do. I will match you, dollar for dollar, on the development work; and then, if we find ore, I would like to run the mine on shares."

"You have thought this all out, eh? You are interested in the Planchas de Plata? Then tell me, my friend, why have you never gone up there and examined it for yourself?"

"If I had," answered Fox, "the people would say I was planning to marry your daughter."

"And you do not wish to do that, eh?"

"No, Señor, I have had enough trouble. I will never trust a woman again."

"Ah! Aha! I begin to understand. You have been very unfortunate, my friend, but all women are not the same.

65

I have been married to my *esposa* for thirty years and she has never turned against me. All the money I have, she knows where it is buried. That is how much I trust my Luz."

He glanced towards the half-door and Fox drew down his lip. He did not trust Doña Luz, himself. She had planned it very nicely to make him marry Elodia—to keep her from becoming an old maid. There was no love, no sentiment, no friendship for him—just the usual Spanish loyalty to her husband and her family. But in everything else she was hard.

"Let us forget about the women," said Juan. "You and your wife know where I stand. If I open up your mine it will be a matter of business. Between you and me—no one else."

"Very well," agreed Gallardo, "and I will accept your proposal. We will share both the profits and the expense. I will match your eight thousand pesos with eight thousand more and give you half of all we make. Shall we write it on a piece of paper?"

"With pleasure," answered Fox, shaking hands to bind the bargain. "But there are one or two things more. The property will remain in your name—but I will have full control of it as long as I am in charge. Whatever I think best I will do, and you can fire me in thirty days."

"But I do not wish to fire you!" protested Don Francisco, laughing. "You are a Yanqui, but I know you are honest. When I ask you a question you give me an answer. All you seek in this country is money—no land, no woman, nothing but gold. And when you get enough you will go back to Arizona. You will return to the

United States."

"That is the idea," admitted Don Juan.

"And you have done nothing from which to hide?"

"No, I just came down to forget."

"Ah the woman! And have you forgotten her?"

"Almost," replied Fox. "But not what she has done. From this time on I look out for Number One. No woman will fool me again."

He glanced towards the half-door, where the Señora was looking out, and Gallardo made haste to intervene.

"Bring me paper and pen!" he cried, clapping his hands. "And a bottle of good old wine! Tomorrow in the morning I will ride into town—we will open up our mine!"

CHAPTER IX

THE CHIEF OF THE *GAMBUSINOS*

WHAT A STIR THERE WAS in old Todos Santos when Francisco Gallardo, with his retinue of armed menservants, rode in to open up the mine! The Planchas de Plata, which had turned out slabs of silver and paid a King's ransom to the Crown! He shook hands affably with Pepe Torres, the Spaniard, and other leading citizens of the town; and then, with his retainers to carry torches and lanterns for him, he led the way to the ancient mine.

It stood on a low, red hill, half-buried in its own dumps like the workings of an industrious gopher; and above it there loomed the volcanic crags which formed the capping of the ore. Along the base of the hill a long, sunken pit marked the spot where the first silver had been dug—the place where those early explorers, making a fire by the trail, had beheld the pure metal run out and mingle with the iron-wood coals.

One fifth of its yield for five years had been paid to the Emperor of Spain for protection against savage foes, but every pound of ore had been carried from its depths on the backs of Indian slaves. Then the Spanish power had waned, revolution had reared its head and the Planchas de Plata, its pillars looted by ore thieves, had caved in and gone to ruin. But François Gaillard, that learned, exiled Frenchman, had opened up new workings above, taking out a fortune in silver before misfortune had driven him insane.

Don Francisco, his son, expatiated at length upon the glories of the past; and Fox could see from his talk that he knew nothing about mines. That in a way was an advantage, for it would give him a free hand in the work. The old men who led the way, holding up torches to light the walls of huge chambers, had helped to carry out the last ore, and now they in turn waxed garrulous; but the *gambusinos* who still prowled those passages at night and carried off picked ore to their *arrastres* were not present except in spirit. Near the portals of the mine, where the last daylight faded away, John Fox spied their shrine with its pictures of the Virgin—and the candle-stumps before it were fresh.

Down the rough stone steps that descended through old stopes they made their way cautiously to narrow passageways, where notched logs led to greater depths—and then they trooped solemnly out again. Nothing had been done, but the mine had been turned over to Don Juan Fox and Gallardo could return to his ranch, where the grinding of his sugar cane demanded attention. Men who professed to be miners but looked more like *gambusinos* applied to the new *jefe* for work, but he told them to come again. He had no steel, no powder to break the ground; and, furthermore, though he did not say so—no ore.

But somebody, he knew, had ore. He had seen pure silver passed over the bar to Pepe Torres, and the men who bought the drinks made no bones of it. They were a desperate *gente,* this clan of *gambusinos;* the best judges of ore-bodies in all Mexico but bad men to meet in a stope. Many a shift boss and inspector had had an ore chute pulled on him or been stabbed by the dagger-like point of a miner's candlestick. An old breed, these ore thieves, passing on from father to son the secrets and subtle wiles of their trade. They would resent any interference with their illicit traffic—but Fox thought he knew a way.

He drank elbow to elbow with these horny-handed men—who paid their counts with silver to try him out— and then he beckoned Torres to one side.

"Let your barkeeper serve the drinks," he said. "We have more important business, no?"

"To be sure!" answered Pepe, seizing a bottle to take with them; and in his private room he poured out the wine.

"Now!" he said, grinning. "You know, eh? I have been crazy to tell you for a week. They have struck ore in the Planchas de Plata!"

"I know it!" nodded Juan. "Are they taking out much?"

"*Mucho!*" exclaimed Torres. "But I begged them to hide it until your contract with Gallardo was signed. If the old man had known how much silver they are spending—"

"I see," said Fox. "But I will divide with Gallardo honestly. A friend is a friend and Don Francisco has given me a good contract. But at the same time, Pepe, we must do this our own way. Do you know a good, honest *gambusino?*"

Pepe emptied his glass and blinked good-naturedly.

"Their chief!" he said. "A wonderful miner—he can smell out ore the way a dog follows a rabbit. But like most of them he has a weakness." And Pepe crooked his elbow.

"So much the better," grinned Fox, "I believe I can use such a man. Why should I break my neck, climbing down those chicken ladders looking for ore? Why not throw in with your friend, the chief ore robber, and pay him for the work? He will do a better job than a hundred mining experts—and besides, I need him in my business."

"Yes?" observed Pepe. "In what way?"

"To protect me from the rest of these ore thieves, if some of them should want to kill me."

"*Seguro!*" Torres assented gravely. "He would be better than a troop of Rurales."

"Enough!" nodded Fox. "Bring him in. I will make him a proposition."

"And if he refuses?"

"Nothing will be said."

Pepe leapt up nimbly and rushed back to the bar and in a minute through the doorway a huge man appeared, bringing the odor of too much mezcal. It was Roque Salas, the chief of the *gambusinos,* and Don Juan had been drinking next to him. His head was small and weasel-eyed but the rest of him was built big from the ground. The bare feet in his scuffed-up sandals might serve as pedestals for a Hercules and his shoulders were massive as a bronze.

"Buenas tardes, amigo," he said with a sly smile and gave Fox his calloused hand.

"This man," began Pepe, "is my friend, Señor Fox. And you are my very good friend. Now what do you wish to say?"

"First," began Fox, "I want to tell Señor Salas of a new method of mining in Arizona. The ore in this camp does not lie in veins but in pockets and lenses—anywhere. So the boss makes a paper with some man he knows—a good man he can trust. Any ore-body that he finds he can work for thirty days, and all the ore is his. But after that it belongs to the company."

"Yes, sir," nodded Salas. "I understand."

"Then," went on Fox, "the company gives this man another piece of paper, and another piece of ground to work on. Would you like to do that with the Planchas?"

The *gambusino* paused and meditated awhile, fixing the new boss with speculative eyes.

"No, Señor," he said at last. "The other men would kill me."

"I will make a paper with them," promised Juan. "If

they are good miners and know how to find ore."

"But the others!" suggested Salas.

"They must keep out. Nobody can enter without a paper signed by me."

"And *me!*" added Roque, suddenly snapping at the point. Something seemed to have clicked in that small, scheming brain and he waited with a glitter in his eyes.

"Well—and you," agreed Fox. " *'Sta bien!*"

The drinks were on Roque Salas that night and he came to work very late. But he came—and Juan saw the ore. It lay at the end of a long drift, so narrow and crooked that the big Mexican could hardly squeeze through. But it was the real thing, native silver in rotten quartz, and with three helpers Salas went to work. With heavy blows from his short hammer he broke the ore down for the others to scrape up and sack, and that night the secret was out. There was ore in the Planchas, the old days were coming back; and Redhead, the new boss, was going to drive a tunnel to cut the vein from the surface.

The crowd around Pepe's bar was almost delirious; and, to add to their astonishment, Redhead bought Salas' ore himself! At the regular ore-buyer's price! In one short shift Roque Salas and his three helpers had made over two hundred pesos. It went, that same night, in the biggest celebration that Todos Santos had seen for years; and the next day Roque was drunk. But the news was out and Gallardo rode in early to gaze at the gleaming ore.

"But what is this I hear?" he demanded at the end. "Are you buying your own ore from these thieving *gambusinos* and paying the regular price? What profit can there be in that?"

72

"None whatever!" answered Fox. "But thirty days is not a long time, and already Roque Salas is dead drunk. At the end of his month the ore-body will be ours and we can open up our mine from the outside. A short tunnel, straight in—we cut the vein and follow it down. And then there will be other veins."

"But shall it be said around the country that Francisco Gallardo has an alliance with ore thieves and robbers? I do not like your smart Yanqui way of finding ore so quick. This Roque Salas is a rascal."

"He is the chief of them all—that is why I hire him—to protect me from the rest. They are afraid of him, and of his three husky sons, and this brother who acts as his hammer-man. Do you want to have me killed?"

"Well—no!" answered Gallardo. "No, no, my dear friend. If you think best you may work your own way. But what a thought—to buy your ore from *gambusinos*—and pay them the regular price!"

"But wait," said Fox, "until I drive that tunnel in and tap, perhaps, new veins of ore. Your father's mine, Señor Gallardo, is not half worked out. We shall soon be rich, you and I."

"So I hope," returned the old man. "But come out to see me often. I wish to be the first, and not the last, to hear of these shrewd Yanqui tricks."

"To be sure," responded Don Juan. "But not right away. I must order drills and powder, clear the assay-office out and hire a mill-man to refit the old mill. And then, you remember, your wife was displeased—"

"But not now—it has all been explained."

"Perhaps!" shrugged Fox. "But this trouble has been a

73

lesson to me."

"No, no! Come!" coaxed Gallardo. "And do not take my Luz too seriously. She is a mother, you know, and nothing would do but I must ask you, straight out, about Elodia. My poor daughter has wept for days, for shame that it should happen. Will you not come out next Sunday, to see her?"

"No, my friend," replied Juan. "I shall be very busy. The tunnel—the mill, my supplies! Everything is needed and nothing is here. But perhaps some other time."

"We will look for you," said Don Pancho hopefully. But he knew Fox would never come.

CHAPTER X

A ONE-PRICE MAN

STRIKE FOLLOWED STRIKE in the Planchas de Plata as ore thief after ore thief took out his *papel* and traced some stringer to its source. Roque Salas, the king of the *gambusinos,* collected tribute from every man; and with all the help in town he could hardly drink up the money. Todos Santos was on the boom and the busiest man of all was John Fox, now called Redhead or *El Patron.*

When the mill was not breaking down or his contractors all getting drunk there were his supply trains and bullion shipments to worry about; and at night, mysteriously, he worked in his assay-office, digging a chamber to hold their treasure. In that land of no banks and many *ladrones* every man had to bury his gold. There had to be a place where he could go to get money or store his bars of silver; but beneath the hearth in front of the furnace he dug a second chamber, unknown even to faithful Fidel.

While the Yaqui sat outside with his rifle across his knees, driving away both the inquisitive and the vicious, Fox raised the square of steel and, night after night, scraped out a little earth. The hole became deeper, big enough to hide a man, and he devised a secret latch which held down the door and could be operated from the inside. There were troublous times in Old Mexico, with a revolution starting in Chihuahua; and some day, over that pass, a band of *revoltosos* might ride in, to rob the rich old mine.

All the treasure of the Planchas was buried in one hole, until it could be smuggled out and converted into pesos. That was the Company's bank, known and approved by Gallardo; the other was a personal hideout. In it Fox stored away his sacks of gold and currency, with bottles of water and food; and when the time came he could either hide there or take his savings and ride for the Line. But now he stood pat, working feverishly day and night to build up a good, big stake. Say a hundred thousand dollars, to pay him for his labors and the indubitable chances he took; for with the Planchas in bonanza he was a marked man in that country and the *ladrones* might get him, any time.

The days ran into weeks and then months, nothing happened except more trouble and more work; and then one afternoon Yermo Gallardo came galloping in and snatched him out of his chair.

"Come quick!" he gasped, "and bring all your medicine. Elodia has been bitten by a *matavenado*. My mother says she is dying."

"Saddle my horse!" ordered Fox and as Fidel ran to obey he got together his medicines. The "deer-killers" were very bad at that season of the year, nearly every week someone was bit, but who would think of it happening to Elodia! He mounted on the run and went spurring up the trail—but he could not believe she was dying. That was just her mother's way of talking. Up the last steep hill, and the race course lay before him. Pardo galloped, leaving the others far behind; and when, at the gate, he fell forward on his knees Juan leapt off and rushed through the crowd.

Within the house there was terrible confusion—women weeping, rushing about, saying their prayers; but the worst of them all was Doña Luz herself. Fox found Elodia buried deep under a load of blankets and gasping for the breath of life, and when he threw them off to get at the wound the Señora burst out in shrill protests. From the torrent of Spanish which poured from her lips Don Juan judged it was some matter of the proprieties and thrust her roughly away.

"Out of my way!" he ordered. "You talk too much, woman!" And Doña Luz retired in a huff. To be called a woman! And by this hard-eyed Yanqui! But Fox ignored her rage. On Elodia's slender leg there was a lump the size of his fist, such a bite as only the deer-killer could inflict. He opened up his kit, thrust the needle through a cork and injected permanganate into the bite. Then he straightened up and looked at Elodia as she lay panting in the hot, close air.

The case had not gone as far as with Marcelina but her lips were twisted in agony, her face was turning black and her throat was fast closing up. He snatched his bottle of turpentine, tore her filmy gown apart and rubbed it on her chest. But even in his haste he could not but note the beauty of her heaving breast, that full virginal beauty of the tropics which before he had only guessed. Perhaps for a moment he forgot his doctor's part—and then Doña Luz leapt upon him.

"Give me that bottle!" she cried. "And take your hands away! I will rub it on, myself!"

Juan looked up, astonished; then to assert his authority he gave her an order instead.

"Go, you!" he said, "and crush me some onions to make a poultice for her throat!"

The Señora flew back and glared at him angrily. He had called her *tu,* that most disrespectful of pronouns used only for menials and familiars! But her daughter's life was at stake and she hurried into the kitchen. Fox worked fast in her absence, squeezing mezcal between Elodia's lips to pick up her lagging heart; but when Luz came running back her daughter was in convulsions and with a shriek she fell on her knees.

"Madre de Dios!" she cried. "She is dying! Nothing can save her!" And all the women set up a wail.

"Give me the onions!" commanded Juan, snatching the pan away. "And get out of here, all you women. I can save her yet—did I not cure Marcelina? But leave the room and give her air!"

He bound the poultice around her neck and as Elodia inhaled the vapors she gasped and drew a deep breath.

"Oh, cure her!" implored Luz. "Name your price—we will pay you well. Only do not let her die!"

Fox gazed at her absently as he felt the faint heartbeats that threatened every moment to stop. Then he opened his bottle of digitalis and forced a tablet down her throat.

"Poor child!" wailed the Señora. "Can nothing be done? She would not let me send for you, not even to save her life. Her pride has brought her to this."

Don Juan wet a piece of cotton with mezcal and squeezed the fiery liquor through her teeth. Then he held Elodia close as a fierce convulsion seized her and her breath became a racking gasp.

"She is dead!" clamored Luz. "There is the death rattle, in her throat."

"It is not!" snarled Fox. "Go away from me, woman!"

And once more he returned to his work. When he looked up the Señora was still talking, and in her tirade he had caught the word "Yanqui." A good word, like *tu*, if spoken with a smile; but otherwise a term of reproach. She was scolding him—demanding his price!

"How much do I want?" he repeated, and his hot hate flashed up against her. Even while her daughter was struggling against death she was haggling—offering him silver, and gold!

"How much?" he yapped. "I am a one-price man. Is she not worth as much as Pepe's daughter?"

"What do you mean?" cried the Señora, aghast; and he took the easiest way to get rid of her.

"I want *her!*" he said. "Nothing less."

He leaned over deliberately and kissed Mariquita and Doña Luz seemed to swoon.

"Pancho!" she screamed. "Come in here and see this Yanqui. He is asking for our daughter."

Fox glanced up grimly as Gallardo hastened in.

"Take this woman away," he said.

"But Pancho!" she insisted. "He has insulted our family. When I asked him what he wanted to save our daughter—"

"I told her I was a one-price man," broke in Juan. "Will you not do as much as Pepe and Maria?"

"You want Elodia?" demanded the old man, staring.

"That is my price—if she lives," answered Fox; and looked at Luz again. Then he turned to Elodia, who had opened her eyes. "Is that not better," he asked, "than to die?"

"Yes!" cried Gallardo, reaching out his hand. "I agree!" And he hurried away.

"And you?" inquired Juan, insultingly.

For a moment the black hate gleamed in Doña Luz's eyes, but at last she bowed her head.

"You do it just to shame me!" she sobbed. "But save her! I agree."

"Then leave us alone!" he commanded; and waved them all from the room.

There was a hush as the jostling crowd left and Fox sat down on the edge of the bed. What a devil she was, this wrangling, prudish mother, always hovering over her daughter to save her from desecrating hands! If his guess was right she had spoiled Elodia's life, but this would hold her a while. She had scratched a Yanqui and found him a Tartar. Now to save her—his dear, suffering Mariquita!

79

He laid his hands on her cheeks and kissed her hot brow, smoothing away the taut lines of pain. Then he leaned over closer and kissed the writhing lips and suddenly she opened her eyes.

"You are mine," he said. "My woman—if you live. Now help me—fight against the poison."

He laid his hands on her breast and at his touch he could feel her heart leap. She knew him, this cruel Redhead who had never come back to her but who loved her in his own Yanqui way, and in the ecstasy of that fierce caress she summoned a twisted smile. Her dark eyes glowed and she settled back on the pillow to battle for her life.

CHAPTER XI

TO SPITE THE CAT

NOTHING CAN BE KEPT SECRET in Mexico where money and women are concerned, and Don Juan's hard bargain soon came out. He had held up his benefactor, the generous Don Francisco, for the body of his daughter, Elodia! For saving her life he had exacted his Yanqui price—to have her, this beautiful girl, for his woman. Her mother had wept and prayed, offering him uncounted silver and gold, but he had claimed *her,* and had his way. But now the poor daughter was very weak from illness, and from the bite of the venomous *matavenado*.

When Fox rode down the street the people turned and looked—the men with a crooked, envious smile, the women with a startled stare. This Yanqui, the Gringo who had gained half the mine! But to have Elodia—and for his woman! Yet he had sworn an oath never to marry her, so her parents had bowed their heads. They had yielded. But what a man, what a devil for women! And what would Elodia do?

A week passed, and every day he rode to Miraflores—but always with his Yaqui at his back and a rifle under his knee. He was afraid, or so it seemed, but Elodia's wound was slow to heal, where she had been bitten by the terrible deer-killer. He rode up to treat her with medicines he had; and each time, before he left, he kissed her on the lips and whispered in her ear. *Que diablo—esta Cabeza Colorado!* He had no fear of man, God or devil; and whatever he wanted, he took. It was their way—these Yanquis from the North.

It was said that Doña Luz had appealed to her four brothers to prevent this disgrace to their name, but Don Francisco had forbidden the Carillos to interfere—although they could be present, of course. The word was that Gallardo, in one way or another, was determined to keep Redhead in the country—to run his mine and manage its affairs—and it was hoped that the American, after taking her for his woman, would relent and marry Elodia.

She was a charming and beautiful woman—a little old, of course, but still only twenty-two—and would make any man a good wife. And if he married her in this way, against the will of her mother, he would get rid of a very nagging mother-in-law. They had had a quarrel, Don Juan and the Señora, when after calling only twice on Elodia, it had been practically demanded that he marry her. For four months after that, Fox had never gone near the girl who had now been delivered into his hands. His woman, to do with as he pleased! But then—he had saved her life.

When she was near the point of death, so it was said, he had kissed her and brought her back. He had held her in his arms and the strength of his body had passed through his hands into hers. And then he had medicines such as only *curanderos* use, cures whose names are not found in the books. Witch medicines, perhaps, as the *medico* had hinted; but there were onions and turpentine, too. And now she was nearly well and making a red dress as if it was to be her wedding.

It was on the Friday before All Saints' Day that Don Juan went to claim his woman, and there was a rush to see what would happen. He was dressed in his best, with a red handkerchief around his neck, and wearing the buckskin *pantalones* that he had won from Bozo Wilson—the Picacho Pants, first fruits of victory over a hostile country and people. And to top them off he wore a fringed buckskin jacket trimmed with snake-skin down the seams. But he turned a wary eye on the men as they passed and his Yaqui held his gun ready to shoot.

At the gate of Miraflores, Fox left Pardo by the bars and strode in through the whole Carillo clan. All her mother's relations, invited or just come to see what was going to take place. Elodia, snatched from death by the Yanqui *curandero* and now called upon to pay, wore a red silk dress, with the markings of a ladybird, and when he entered she gave him a smile. But Doña Luz and her four brothers never moved from their chairs. Only Gallardo and his daughter did the honors.

"Let me see your leg," said Don Juan brusquely; and while her mother bit her lips he felt the place where the bite had been. "It is cured," he said, and patted her on the knee before he put down her foot.

"Yes," she said and smiled expectantly.

"Don Francisco," he began. "Do you remember the bargain that we made when your daughter was bitten by the *matavenado?* A hard bargain, perhaps, but you remember it?"

"*Sí, Señor,*" responded Gallardo, gravely.

"And you, Señora?" he asked. "Do you remember, too?"

"Yes, I do!" she snapped. "I made it to save my daughter's life!"

"Enough!" he broke in, cutting her short; and went over to where Elodia was waiting. She was very beautiful in her scarlet gown and her eyes as they met his had a glow in their dark depths that told him she was his. But for a moment he seemed at loss for words.

"Mariquita," he said, at last, "you know the bargain your parents made when you were bitten by the *matavenado?*"

"Yes," she said, blushing and looking down. "You saved my life. I belong to you."

"Then come over here," he said, "and give me a kiss. I am sorry it must be our last."

All the crowd was still as death as Elodia started towards him, suddenly halting as she heard his last words. But she went on obediently and when he swept her into his arms she gave him a lover's kiss.

"Another!" he demanded, and as she kissed him again he put her away with a sigh.

"Sweetheart," he said, "I have done this only to try you—and to spite your cat of a mother. Now I am sorry for us both. But I respect you too much to take you for my woman—and as I have said I will marry no one. So I give you back to your father."

He spoke rapidly, looking around at the grim-faced Carillos who had gathered, perhaps, to kill him. Then he clapped on his hat, made a run for the gate and vaulted into the saddle. All the people stared after him as he galloped away and several hot-heads mounted to follow, but when Fidel stopped and held up his hand they changed their minds and rode back.

All was confusion, with the Carillo clan swearing vengeance and Doña Luz carried away in a swoon, but there was nothing to be done. The crazy Yanqui had tricked them again and Elodia broke down and wept.

If he had taken her as he had threatened, her kinfolks could ride after him to save her from that shame; but he had given her back, not without a kiss, and called her mother a cat. It was that, and the knowledge that she had been flouted again, which threw the Señora into her swoon; but her four stout brothers and all their fighting sons could do nothing about it now. The Americano was gone.

He had disappeared down the trail and, the next day being the Fiesta of All the Saints, nobody took the pains to follow. There were Masses and processions before the old church and firing of the cannon from the hill; and then horse races and shooting contests, chicken-pulls and general gayety, with a Grand Ball that lasted all night. All the saints in the calendar were the patrons of Todos Santos; and that fortunate town, now turning out huge bars of silver, celebrated its Saints' Day in style.

But in all the *cantinas* where the Carillo brothers drank there was mention of a hereafter for the Gringo, this red-headed Yanqui who had come in from nowhere and had the effrontery to pay court to their niece. To save her life it had been necessary for Doña Luz to promise anything, even her daughter's hand; but if he had dared to claim Elodia he would never have got to town. They would have killed him on the road. Or so they said.

But Don Juan did not return and, after sobering up, the brothers Carillo went back to their ranches. Todos Santos sobered up and, still feeling a little *crudo,* the foreman opened the mine whose silver was the lifeblood of the town. It was then that, for the first time, the Red-head was really missed; for someone dropped a sledge hammer into the rock-crusher of the mill and left it a total wreck. Then Roque Salas killed two men in the mine and the Planchas de Plata closed down.

LIBERTY AND JUSTICE

CHAPTER XII

THE ARMY OF LIBERATION

Todos Santos was an ancient and prosperous town, with all the saints to pray to and the Planchas de Plata to live on—but without two men it was nothing. Roque Salas, the chief of the *gambusinos,* was gone with the Rurales on his trail; and without his heavy hand to restrain them the ore thieves at the mine ran wild. And without Redhead not a wheel could turn. There was no one to take his place.

On the second day, Don Francisco rode to town with his son and posted a heavy guard at the portals of the mine. But the ore thieves had secret entrances, known only to their kind, and they swarmed in to rob the rich stopes. Within a week every outlaw *arrastre* in the country was grinding the pick of the ore, although the company's mill was closed. Gallardo moved to town and brought his family with him, the better to look after his interests. They opened up their old town house and Doña Luz invited her friends in, but no one would hear a word against Don Juan. All they hoped was that the Redhead would come back.

What was it to them—and to the poor, starving miners—that he had tried to get Elodia for his woman? She had been willing, so it was said, but he loved her too much to disgrace her. Was that such a crime—and in a Yanqui? There were girls in Todos Santos who would have him, and gladly. No, no, Doña Luz talked entirely too much. She had driven him away with her tongue.

And now once more Dame Rumor became busy—for all had not been told of this affair. Elodia lived apart in the ancestral home, refusing to be ruled by her mother, and strange things were reported by the servants. On the day she was bitten she had been seen wandering about as if looking for something on the ground. Perhaps a *matavenado*—who could say? And when she found one, being afflicted with the lovesickness, she let it bite her purposely in order to bring him back.

In the extremity of her lovesickness, which was wasting her away, she had preferred a quick death from the deer-killer to enduring her pangs to the end. Either that or to be cured at his hands, and perhaps win him back again. But after the bite, being angry with her mother, she had refused to have Redhead called; and only the quick work of her brother had saved her from becoming a suicide. She must have intended this, or some greater sin, for she had refused to attend the confessional. Nor would she go to church, except in the early morning when only the maidservants were abroad.

Three long weeks of feminine speculation and masculine hope and despair were brought to an end at last when Don Juan was discovered in the assay-office one morning, peacefully testing some samples of ore. It was the sight of Fidel on the doorstep with his rifle across his knees that guided Don Francisco to the spot, and he alone was let in. *El Patron* had some business to settle— a little money to divide before he quit. But Gallardo rushed in and gave him the *embrazo* as if he were a long-lost son.

"Ah, Don Juan!" he cried, "you have come just in time. But where have you been all these weeks?"

"Out prospecting," answered Redhead, "and hiding from the Carillos. Here is some very good ore I found."

"The Carillos!" echoed Gallardo. "And why should you hide from them? All that is forgotten—my wife's people have gone home. Doña Luz has confessed she was wrong."

"In what way?" inquired Juan.

"She sees now, my boy, that it was all a joke. You had no intention of doing Elodia a wrong. It was only in Luz's mind."

"Perhaps so," admitted Fox. "She hates me, that I know. But Don Pancho, it is time we closed our affairs and divided up the money we have earned. I am going back to Arizona."

"What? And leave me with the mine? I cannot begin to handle it. I know nothing of mining or of miners. Ever since you left, the mill has been closed down and Roque Salas killed two men."

"I am sorry," said Don Juan. "But I have been here long enough. And now I am ashamed to look Elodia in the face, so it is best to go away."

"But no!" protested Gallardo, laughing and patting him on the back. "You have done nothing she will not forgive. Many other girls have said they envied her such a lover—a man who would do her no wrong."

"It was not right," confessed Fox. "I see it all now. But Doña Luz brings out the worst in my nature. To her I am always a damned Yanqui, who thinks of nothing but money."

"It is her way," smiled Don Pancho. "Do not notice it too much. For thirty years she has been a true and loyal wife, and she has promised to say no more. So please stay, my friend, and help me with the mine before everything is lost."

"Well," said Juan at last, after listening to many arguments. "I will stay, then—a little while."

"If only for a day!" pleaded Gallardo. And so the

Patron came back. On the first day he told the gang to quit trying to mend the rock-crusher and to break the ore by hand. Then he sent out for new parts and went up to the mine, where Yermo stood guard at the door. Not a pound of ore was coming up from the depths, for the miners were afraid to work. The *gambusinos* had taken charge, slipping in at their secret entrances and driving the contractors out—and Redhead left them alone.

"We must get back Roque Salas," he decided. "I will see the captain of the Rurales."

Two days later the doughty Roque came back and his case was declared self-defense. The men he had killed had invaded the Planchas property and attempted to drive him out and he had stabbed them with his candle-stick. Or that is what he told the summary court which the Rurales have power to hold, and both the other witnesses were dead. Nevertheless he was grateful to the *Patron,* who had saved him from the fusillade; and when he walked out, a free man, all but the boldest of the *gambusinos* fled.

The mine opened up full blast again, the mill turned out silver as before; but there was something sinister about this shut-down which Fox would not soon forget. There was an element in the town and in the mine that was growing more defiant every day; and these men it was who had taken over the stopes the minute his back was turned. They had lost all respect for authority and law. Only his guns and Roque's dagger could control them.

It was time, he could see, to close up his affairs, take his money and start for the Line. For beneath all this freebooting and defiance of the law there could be heard the mutterings of revolt. The hand of Porfirio Diaz was weakening, though his Rurales still executed his will, and men in their cups were heard to mutter of a day when all peons would be free. There would be, on that Day, no servants and no masters. And when it came Fox wanted to be gone.

A revolution was brewing, he could read the signs. He had made a stake—so why not go? Step out some dark night without saying good-by and keep moving until he crossed the Line. His hunch was good and he would have followed it right then, except for Mariquita's handkerchief. She dropped it through the bars that evening as he was passing beneath her window, and old habit made him pick it up. Then he saw her smiling eyes looking out at him and the revolution was forgotten.

"Ah! Aha!" she laughed. "Did you know it was I? Or did you hope to see a fairer face?"

"I know nothing!" he answered, "except that something here bids me hand it back and be gone!"

"Then I will take it!" she pouted; but as their hands met they clutched and he felt all his resistance ebb away.

"Let me go," he whispered huskily, "before I climb up and kiss you!"

"I dare you!" she challenged, leaning close; and he swung up and claimed his meed.

"*Madre de Dios!*" he muttered as he clung there. "If your mother should see me now!"

"But no!" she said. "She is my mother no more. Did you not give me back to my father?"

"To be sure! How forgetful I am getting! And Don

Francisco was always my friend!"

"He is so still, for he left the gate unlocked and the porter has gone for a drink."

She gazed at him, daringly, and Don Juan fell, though his heart told him he would rue the day. He dropped down lightly and slipped through the gate, then turned and glided into her room.

"My sweetheart!" she sighed as he clasped her in his arms. "Have you decided to forgive me at last?"

"And for what?" he asked, still kissing her.

"For being like that girl who has poisoned your life and turned you against all women. Oh, tell me before you go—for you must not stay long—what kind of a creature was she? Was she tall or short? A blond or a brunette? How can I hate her unless I know what she is like?"

"Like a short, fat blond, then," he grumbled.

"Then she is not like me—at all!"

"Not at all! The very opposite!"

"And did she not love you?"

"She said so."

"You mean," she cried, pushing him away, "that all women are the same?"

"Perhaps," he replied. "I shall never be sure. What would happen to me now if your mother should find me? I am barred in—there is no way out."

"Yes—this way!" she said, taking him resolutely by the arm and thrusting him out the door. "When have I ever offered to betray you, Gringo? But go now, before someone comes!"

She shut the door in his face and, after thinking a minute, Don Juan went his way. That was not the place for a young gentleman to be found unless he wished to marry the girl. And as for that, he would marry no one. All he asked of Mexico was to get out of the country before it was everlastingly too late.

But in the morning it was too late. They marched in from the north, as sorry a looking band of *pelados* as Redhead had ever seen, but revolutionists with ribbons on their hats. Red, white and green, instead of the eagle and snake of Diaz. The Day had come and when they halted in the Plaza for their leader to make a speech, Fox listened to him curiously. He was Juan de Dios Campo, a miner from Cananea and an agitator of the harmless type. A follower of Madero, the dreamer, whose little book he held in his hand.

But the men behind him! Cananea had been a hotbed of rebellion since the riots of 1906, and most of these *hombres* could handle dynamite. Only the arrest of their radical chief had put Campo at their head. They would be a tough gang to handle if they once got started—and there was that bullion, buried under the floor. Campo had mounted the band-stand to make his speech, which seemed to have no end, and his followers sat down to rest their feet. Not one in a hundred was armed and only the officers had horses, but they were men to be handled with gloves.

Campo spoke on the Plan of San Luis Potosi, Madero's Declaration of Rights and also his Call to Arms; and then, walking over to the Company Store, he asked for food for his men.

"No, sir!" began Gallardo, confronting him defiantly; but Redhead pushed him gently aside and beckoned the general in.

"To be sure!" he responded. "Your followers look like good men—and miners, like ourselves. Here are beans and corn, and jerked beef; and some canned goods to make a quick meal. Is there anything else you would like?"

"Some matches and cigarettes—we are all out of tobacco—"

"*Orita*—right away!" spoke up Don Juan briskly. "Send in ten men and I will give them all you want. It is hard to go without a smoke."

General Campo stepped out and a hundred men answered his call, but Fox ordered his clerks to hand out the supplies until even the hungriest was satisfied. Then he guided them to the camp-ground and gave them a load of wood and left them to break their long fast.

"Who are those men?" demanded the townspeople anxiously, as Fox rode back to the store. "Where are they going? Will they attack us?"

"Not if we feed them—and keep them from getting drunk. They are part of the Army of Liberation which has risen up all over Mexico and they are marching over the mountains to Chihuahua to join Madero and Cruz Pizano."

"Cruz Pizano!" roared Gallardo. "That robber? That bandit? Then I shall refuse to give them anything."

"Do so," answered Fox, "and they will take it anyhow and rob every house in town. We must think, Don Pancho, of the women and children. And if we feed these *pelados* they will soon go on."

He hurried inside to hide the guns and ammunition and

to order more food sent down. Then he ordered Roque Salas to take all the dynamite and conceal it in an abandoned stope.

"What are you going to do now?" demanded Gallardo as Juan took down clothes from the shelves. "Is it not enough to feed these *bandidos* without replacing their worthless rags? You are a good man, Juanito, at running a mine, but these people you do not understand!"

"Perhaps not!" responded Fox. "We will talk that over later. But with your permission I will give them these clothes before they come and take them."

Once more the wagons were loaded up and sent racing down to the camp and when Juan de Dios Campo saw the piles of new hats, the bales of overalls and jumpers, he came over to Redhead and shook hands.

"My friend," he said, "I saw you listening, very attentively, while I made my speech in the Plaza; and I thank you for these supplies. You are an American—you understand when I speak of Liberty and Justice, Effective Suffrage and No Reëlection. I will give you a receipt and when our Cause has been won you will be paid for everything, in full!"

"A thousand thanks," bowed Fox, "if you wish to pay. I will have my clerk send down the bill and your name on it will be enough."

He took the piece of paper and folded it away carefully—but when the Army of Liberation had gone he threw it into the fire. Half the shelves in the Store were empty but the thunder of the stamps had never ceased. The Planchas de Plata was still turning out ore, and one day's run would pay it all back.

CHAPTER XIII

MEXICO!

THE RAG-TAG ARMY OF JUAN DE DIOS CAMPO passed on into turbulent Chihuahua and there came back news of fighting, but Todos Santos paid no great heed. The *revoltosos* had taken a few horses from the ranches, and the Company had given them some clothes, but when they left they had taken also forty or fifty saloon bums whose presence would never be missed. They were ore thieves, trouble-makers, the ne'er-do-wells of the community, and if the Rurales happened to kill them—what matter?

Redhead restocked his store, hid his guns and ammunition and waited for the next army to come. The country was in a tumult, the people were taking sides; but it was the same old division which had always existed—the rich against the poor. The Porfiristas, adherents of Porfirio Diaz, were the landowners, the officeholders, the people of wealth and influence. But those who had nothing, the humble *pelados,* or plucked ones, were for Madero, though to them he was only a name. They were against the reëlection of Diaz, against his soldiers and the Rural Police—against all who had more than they.

Fox felt the change in the attitude of his men, and he thought he sensed also a general apathy on the part of the Government; but there was no way of getting news. He knew nothing—less than nothing—hearing only the senseless chatter of a people crazed by hatred and fear. It was said that thousands and thousands of Maderistas were being executed all over the land, but that in many other districts the peons had risen up, killed the landlords and taken everything.

Only one thing was certain—the trails were not safe to travel and it was not time for the Gringo to make his get-away. With every fresh rumor of advancing hosts the town filled up with fugitives—the women-folks of rich *hacendados,* who had remained behind to protect their property. Gallardo's big house was so crowded with Car-illos that Fox no longer passed by. They were a jealous crew, these *cuñados* and *parientes* of Doña Luz, and a dainty handkerchief dropped from the window might be followed by a bullet—or a laugh.

But even in times of war these daughters of Old Mexico did not forget their main purpose in life. In the Plaza at night, while the big bass viol beat time for the cornet and flute, they appeared beneath the lights like white moths and the boys marched past them to look. In pairs and giggling groups, their arms entwined, their eyes ever seeking some admiring glance, they paced round and round, each looking for her mate while vast armies prepared to deal death.

Elodia was there too, as flirtatious as the rest but more lovely in her China silk gowns. Red she wore, the color of her embodiment, the color that had lured him once before; but now Don Juan gazed on her coldly. It was best to let her marry some Mex. Some strapping *hacen-dado's* son, like this swarm of Carillos that stood between him and a word with her. Only better, more worthy of her love. Let her marry and settle down to have a home and children, before the evil day came when these marching armies locked in battle. For a woman like her, Todos Santos was no place to live—no place for any woman to live.

But she strolled on with the rest, while furtively, across the space, red roses fell at her feet. The Mexican never lived who could gaze on Mariquita without responding to her allure. She was so graceful, so charming with that glow in her dark hair and the flame of Chinese red at her throat—and that deeper flame in the depth of her black eyes when she looked at him, across the space! But no, Juan had made up his mind.

What a life for a white man to live—even with her—in a land like this! In Old Mexico, with its outlaws, its peons, its agitators—and always some new kind of hell. Today it was Madero with his Liberty and Justice, his marching armies of homeless *pelados*. Tomorrow it would be some new and sterner man, mowing them down, standing them up against the wall. Black Indians, low-browed *mestizos,* all breeds and no breeds, but filled with the same urge to kill.

And now, beyond a doubt, there was an army to the south that would soon give them a taste of war—Tiburcio Sanchez, not so long ago a bandit but now all for Liberty and Justice! He could not read or write so there would be no long speeches, no reading of dull documents in the square; but word came every day that he was moving closer, stealing horses, forcing the young men to join. And for those who resisted he had an answer—the same answer that Diaz's Rurales gave to any that opposed his will.

In the hole beneath the furnace in his assay-office, Fox had a fortune stored away. Now that the trails were watched and no shipments could get through, he had taken his share in silver bars. There were enough in that one hiding place to load a mule, and no one knew it was there. Not even Francisco Gallardo, who had greater treasures hidden away. But everybody knew they had money buried somewhere, and in that their danger lay.

There was nothing to do but meet the bandits pleasantly, feed them well and pass them on; and when the great Day of the Porfiristas came—well, some of them would die against the wall. But how to make Don Francisco see this very obvious thing was something not easy to do. He was an aristocrat of the aristocrats—a Cientifico, a friend of Diaz—and for a *mozo* to speak to him without removing his hat was like Ajax defying the lightning. But the time had gone by for all that.

As for Fox, he was still Cabeza Colorado but no longer *El Patron.* The people still loved him for curing Marcelina—for opening up the mine—for giving them work; but the treacherous *gambusinos* who had seized it in his absence were waiting for a chance to strike back. He had loosed upon them—after he had fled from the Rurales—the weasel-eyed, ruthless Roque Salas; and, denied their traditional right to steal from the mine, they were fit for treason, stratagems and spoils. And when Tiburcio Sanchez came to town they would rise up and make their complaints.

He rode in at dawn, a tall, arrogant man with his hair plastered down across his forehead; but before him, whooping and yelling and firing their guns into the air, came a detachment of his *vaquero* scouts. They clattered through the square and out the other side, to cut off any attempts at escape; and the mothers of sons began to weep. Then, mounted on a blooded horse and followed by his bandit friends, Sanchez galloped up in front of the town hall, where the *Presidente* and council awaited him.

"Hombres," he said boldly, "I am a friend of the common people. I have nothing to do with you. Open your doors when my men give the order or they will break them down and kill you."

He turned to his army and waved his arm in a wide circle like the *mayordomo* in charge of a round-up.

"Bring every man—*here!*" he said, and touched the horn of his saddle.

Squads of men rode up every street, banging the doors with the butts of their rifles, and soon in the broad plaza the citizens of Todos Santos gathered to hear the next word of this General.

"Let every man step out who is married or working in the mine. I hate the *ricos,* who wring huge profits from the sweat of the people, but it is necessary that the mine should run."

"Viva!" shouted the miners, stepping forward; and Sanchez beckoned to Fox.

"Is this one of your men?" he asked as the procession passed by; and wherever he could Redhead nodded. He knew what would follow next.

"Now, you young men!" challenged Sanchez, waving his rifle, "your country needs your services. I offer you a place in my army, which is marching to fight Diaz in Chihuahua, and I will give every man a horse and a gun and this ribbon to wear on his hat. Besides that you will have the best of everything, for my soldiers are my friends. Do not molest the women unless they are willing, but the drinks and food are free. In every town I will open the stores to you. Now step forward—every man who will join!"

Some hesitated and held back, but they knew the alternative and all joined. It was better than standing up against the pitted wall of the jail—and besides, the drinks were free. Pepe Torres looked down his nose, but he set out the bottles; and Redhead took a receipt for everything in the commissary from this bandit friend of the people. The Company store was looted from top to bottom, and what they could not use they packed off on the mules which were requisitioned from every ranch.

The proud Carillos, who had made such boasts, were compelled to bring in their herds; but crafty Don Pancho had driven his into the mountains a month or more before. It went hard to see his store stripped of everything, but two of the Carillos had been threatened with death and he had learned to hold his tongue. At last the Army of Liberation marched away up the canyon, shouting *vivas* for *Libertad* and *Justicia,* and many young men came out of hiding. When he knew they were surely gone, Redhead tore up his receipt—and Gallardo stamped it into the dust.

"Is this Liberty?" he cried. "Is this Justice?"

"Quien sabe," shrugged Juan. "It is Mexico."

CHAPTER XIV

LOVESICKNESS

THEY ARE GONE!" railed Gallardo, shaking his fist at the army's dust. "They have gone the way of my two sons—and for the same reason. Nobody would have them around. The scum of the country, without even the brains to work. But now they are out of the way!"

"Perhaps!" said Don Juan. "But where will this end? The next army that comes through may demand our money—or the silver from the mine."

"They will never get it from me!" answered Don Pancho firmly. "I will hold out till I die."

"Why not dig it up, arm our friends with the guns we have hid, and make a break for the Line?"

"And leave everything to these low *pelados?*"

"That is better than to die," replied Juan.

"Ah, my friend," exclaimed Gallardo, "you do not know my people if you think we will yield so weakly. The Spanish and the French both know the value of money. They pass it on from father to son, and I still have my Yermo left. A fine boy, a brave boy! Shall I leave him with nothing? And then, you have forgotten Elodia."

"Well, maybe," shrugged Fox. "She is a beautiful woman, no? Such a woman as a soldier might like. What would you say if some bandit General asked for her? Is it not better to take her to the Line?"

"Ah!" said the old man, smiling slyly. "You still think of my daughter, eh? Then let me tell you, Don Juan, the man who marries her inherits half of all I possess. I have much—perhaps more than you think."

"Perhaps so," admitted Juan. "But I am not minded to marry. And if I were, Don Francisco, the money would make no difference. She is enough in herself, without that."

"My boy," beamed Gallardo, "I want you to talk with her. Yes, yes, you must come. And now! Have I ever denied you when you have asked me a favor? Then grant me this one! Come and see her!"

"And be held up by her mother!"

"She has no mother now. Doña Luz has agreed. But Elodia must see you—now!"

"About what?" demanded Don Juan.

"She will tell you," he wheedled. "A matter of great importance. Perhaps she will leave, as you say."

He took him gently by the arm and led him through the door of his house and at a glance all the servants disappeared. Doña Luz and the Carillos dropped quickly out of sight, for Gallardo was master here. He left Fox in the room where he had met Elodia before, and while he was steeling himself for the interview she suddenly appeared before him.

"Have I offended you?" she asked him gently. "Do you no longer wish to see me? Day and night I ask myself that question!"

"No, sweetheart," he answered. "I say No to both your questions. You have not offended me and I do not wish to see you. It is better, since I can never marry you."

"But why," she said quietly, "can you never marry me? Please tell me, to set my mind at rest. Ah, Juan, have you never felt the pangs of lovesickness? Is it nothing to you that I suffer?"

"I am sorry if you suffer," he replied. "But I told you from the first—I will never marry you or any woman."

"Yes, but what did she do, this other woman? Was she unfaithful? I wish to know."

"Very well," he said, "I will tell you, since I may leave here anytime. What she did was very little. The way she did it was what hurt. I will tell you and have it over—she married the other man. I had bought the house, I had bought all the furniture, I was down at the station to meet her. Then the operator gave me a telegram. She had married a man at home. Rather than come to Arizona and live in a mining camp she married a clerk in a store."

"But I would follow you anywhere," said Elodia, smiling wistfully. "I am your woman. Your love is everything."

"That may be so, but I am not going to marry you. I have given you back to your father. Get some more pretty clothes and make eyes at the *amantes*—I see them all watching you as they pass."

Elodia laughed and sank down in a chair while he still stood warily erect.

"I am not wearing the pretty clothes to catch some foolish young *amante*. They are all afraid to stand beneath my window—they know I belong to you. Since you saved me from the *matavenado* I am yours, to do with as you will. And perhaps, who knows, you are the only man left who wants to have an old maid. But is

103

twenty-two so old?"

"Not in my country. It is nothing. We live a long time. But damn it, Mariquita, *she* was just twenty-two when she quit me and married this dub—a little stoop-shouldered fellow—any kind of a man to keep from leaving home. All she thought of was her people, and living soft at home. And there I was in Arizona with a house and all the furniture—and a ring! And all the boys down at the station to see the bride arrive. I stepped up on the same train and rode it south, and here I am."

"Poor boy!" sighed Elodia, rising up and coming closer, "I hate her too—for making me an old maid. But there is nothing to be done. Just live—and if I die, no matter. That is all, Juan. You may go."

She eyed him with a smile which turned into an anguished twist as he bowed and went quickly out. If he stayed, if he tried to comfort her, one kiss would make him forget. She was his woman, perhaps, but he had not taken her for his woman. He would not marry at all. And if all the young *amantes* were afraid, he would go away then and let them play bear. Let them stand beneath her window until—in no great time, perhaps—she listened and married one of them. Some Mex who had heard of Gallardo's promise and would marry her for her dowry.

Going home Juan remembered the story of the American who had married a Mexican Señorita who had brought him as a dowry ten hairless dogs and one thousand *cuñados* or brothers-in-law—and Mexican relations could be hell. There were the Carillos, for instance. But he was not going to marry into their clan. He was not going to settle down in that land of *Mañana* and live on chili-pepper until the coyotes would not eat him. That is, when he got killed in some revolution, and left his bones to bleach in the sun.

No! He had come down to make a stake and he had it buried, right now, under the floor of his assay-office. The time to go had come and he was balancing his accounts when Gallardo slipped in at the door.

"No?" he queried brokenly. "You could not agree? And now you are going away? Ah, Juan, you are like a son. You have been a son to me. How can I bear to have you leave!"

He burst into tears and as Fox rose up he hugged him and gave him the *embrazo*.

"But very well," he went on. "I will not say a word, for the times are becoming dangerous. Only when you go I shall add to your half a half more from what was my share. That is to show how I love you—and how I would welcome you back."

"No, no!" protested Juan, patting him on the back affectionately. "You have given me too much already. The Planchas has made me rich. But if I stay, some bandit will put me against the wall and force me to give it all up. I know how they do in Durango and Chihuahua, and I know when I have enough. I just came to this country to make a stake and if I stay I will lose it all."

"But Don Juan," reasoned Gallardo, "the two armies have both passed, one from the north and one from the south. All our low, discontented ones have gone over into Chihuahua and none of them will ever come back. This Colonel Rabigan has been concentrating his troops at Casas Grandes. And besides him there are all the

Rurales. They have been withdrawn from here to attack that base rabble and kill them, every one. Only stay and you will hear of the great victory that is coming—and after that there will be peace."

"Well—maybe," admitted Fox. "But this is not my war. I do not belong in this country, and yet I know if I stay here I will be drawn into it and probably killed. Only yesterday when Tiburcio Sanchez asked me to give him my two pistols—"

"I had not heard of that!" exclaimed Don Pancho.

" 'I will take those two *pistolas*,' he said. 'They will look very well, in place of these.'

" 'No, my General,' I said. 'These pistols are mine and I am an American citizen. If you kill me to take them, the United States of America will send down an army to punish you.'

"So he thought awhile and decided to let me keep them. But the next General might decide the other way and then I would have to kill him."

"And would you kill him to save your guns?"

"That is what I told Sanchez," answered Juan. "But no man knows how he will act."

"Then stay here and fight for our mine," entreated Gallardo. "That is something to die for—the Planchas!"

"Sure!" laughed Fox. "But I do not want to die. I want to live, and get out of this country. And another thing, Don Pancho, I have been talking with your daughter and I think it best to go. When I drove away her brothers it was so that she could get married, so the young men would feel free to court her. But now these poor boys are afraid of *me*—more afraid than they were of Bizco."

"Ha, ha!" chuckled Gallardo, putting his arm around Juan, "you are a good man, my boy. I am proud of you. When you drove those two away you tried to fill their place. You have been to me like a true son. Now how can I bear to lose you?"

"Well—for a week then—or two weeks. Until we hear from Chihuahua."

When he heard it was everlastingly too late.

CHAPTER XV

THE ARMY OF DEFEAT

THE NEWS CAME FROM CHIHUAHUA that a great battle was being fought. For three days at Casas Grandes the united Army of Liberation attacked Rabigan and his hated *pelones* and on the last day the great victory was won. Madero and Cruz Pizano charged the garrison recklessly and then the masked guns did their work. Machine guns mowed them down, they were drawn into a trap, and the one-pounders burst shells over their heads.

They ran and the Federal cavalry swung open the *cuartel* gates and charged. Until dark they galloped after the scattered *revoltosos,* cutting them down with their flashing sabers, shooting the fugitives, taking no prisoners; while behind them the ghoulish *soldaderas,* the women of the *pelones,* killed the wounded and robbed the dead. There was no quarter, no mercy; and when the cavalry turned back the Rurales took up the chase.

The first fugitives came streaming down through the

pass with the fear of death in their eyes; and for a stack of tortillas, a drink at the bar, they spoke a few words and spurred on. Back into the Hot Country where they had listened to wild-eyed agitators and "generals," where they had been promised their pick of all the women in Chihuahua and all the loot they could carry. Now they came back empty-handed and, still ringing in their ears, was the *pop, pop* of army pistols in the hands of scrawny *soldaderas,* giving the mercy-shot to their wounded companions. The Maderistas were whipped, the great battle was over, and Gallardo walked the streets, exulting.

But this was not the end—only the beginning. A few days later while the mill was running full blast and the miners were down in the stopes, an Army of Defeat swept down through the pass and took possession of the town. They were Red Flaggers, *Colorados*—fighting for nobody, now that Madero was gone—and at the head of their column a blood-red flag declared no quarter and war to the death. They were defeated, embittered, out for revenge on the hated Sonorans, and Cruz Pizano rode at their head.

He had come unawares on peaceful Todos Santos, his big-hatted Chihuahua bandits tailing on to the string of fugitives that had been pouring over the pass for days. It was their high-topped sombreros with wide, slouching rims which had first drawn attention to his men, and by that time they had surrounded the town. Then with a yell and a volley of shots Pizano charged into the Plaza, and the women hid in terror.

There was a hush as the bandit chief drew up in front of the jail, shouting orders in his harsh, Chihuahua voice;

and then the search of the town began. His men seemed to know where every rich man lived, for after the round-up it was seen that not a *rico* had escaped. Gallardo was there; and old Castro, the miser; and Pepe Torres and Redhead, the foreigner—and Pizano looked them over grimly.

He was a tall, hook-nosed man with a saturnine cast of countenance; and he wasted no time on words.

"Devourers of the poor," he began, "I have heard of you, even over in Chihuahua. How you work your men from daylight to dark for three *reales* a day. Thirty-seven centavos! And overcharge them at the store. But now you are called to an account. I want a hundred thousand pesos as a contribution to the Cause. And if you do not raise it quickly I will dynamite your mine and turn my men loose on your town."

He drew his mouth up on one side, peeling his teeth like a wolf, and after a silence Fox spoke to Torres.

"We must pay," he said in English. "How much shall I put you down for?"

"A thousand," answered Pepe; and Pizano's eagle eyes were fixed upon them.

"I have a list," he said, "of every man in town, and how much he should pay. You, Torres, will contribute five thousand pesos; and the Planchas Mine, twenty thousand."

"Five!" cried Pepe. "I am only a poor hotelkeeper—"

"Enough!" rapped out Pizano.

"And a Spanish citizen!" he ended.

"No difference!" snarled the General. "You will pay or be executed. It is the Spanish who have enslaved my people. Put this man in jail!"

Two soldiers stepped forward and as Pepe was whisked away Pizano beckoned to Fox.

"Will you pay me twenty thousand?" he asked.

"Sí Señor!" responded Don Juan promptly; but as he spoke Gallardo rushed up.

"No!" he shouted angrily. "The mine belongs to me. This American is only my manager."

"No difference," ruled Pizano. "He must pay or go to jail." And he jerked his thumb towards the door.

Within half an hour every *rico* in Todos Santos was shut up in the courtyard of the jail, and while Fox stood silent, eyeing the rough guards at the gate, the place became a babel.

"I have nothing—nothing!" wailed old Castro. "How can I pay ten thousand pesos?"

"I will not pay a centavo!" declared Gallardo, over and over. "I will not pay if they kill me!"

"Never mind!" said Pepe as Fox shook his head. "These bandits are all the same. They demand a hundred thousand and go away with ten. The Rurales are not far behind."

He winked knowingly and Juan understood that each side was playing a game. Cruz Pizano was being pursued by the victorious Federals. He was in haste, so he threatened to kill them. But the *ricos* had been through such scenes before and each man was sparring for time. Old Castro's wails became louder, Gallardo seemed out of his head, the rest were clamorous with their protests; but Pizano ignored them scornfully. He too had been through all this before and, as soon as he had taken over the office of the jail, he sent more men through the town. Then the thunder of the mill ceased abruptly and several prisoners were hurried in from the mine. Fox saw Roque Salas with his arms tied behind him standing humbly before his General and Judge and suddenly the false clamor was hushed.

A firing squad, with red rags on their sleeves, came marching into the yard and without a word Salas was stood against the wall. His drink-flushed face became pale with fright, there was a questioning gleam in his eyes and he started as the lieutenant raised his sword. Then with a sharp order the blade flashed down and five guns went off at once. Roque tumbled over backwards as the bullets struck him and fell in a twitching heap.

"Bring me out Cipriano Castro!" shouted Pizano; and Juan saw he had run into war. War as the Mexicans understood it, with no quarter asked or given, no law but the muzzle of a gun. Pizano was an outlaw already, with a price on his head in Chihuahua, and he wore a red ribbon on his sleeve. He had been trapped by Rabigan, drawn into an ambush and half his men left on the field. What to him were the outcries of a village miser, protesting that he had no money? Pizano listened a minute, asked a question or two, and at a sign one of his men brought a rope.

"Listen!" he commanded as the poor old man trembled and fell silent, "you have money, buried beneath the floor of your house. Will you bring it or shall I hang you?"

"No! No!" began Castro; and the loop was clapped over his head. There was a jerk as he was swung up to the gateway of the jail and suddenly he hung writhing in mid-air.

"Down!" motioned Pizano; and waited until the miser could speak.

"Son of a Spanish dog!" he cursed, "do you think I am playing a game? Do you think I know nothing of your misdeeds? For years you have kept these poor people in slavery while your interest ate them up. Now dig up that money or I will hang you to your gate post as a warning to all *ricos* and their wives."

He motioned him away and turned to the jail yard, where the rest of his prisoners stood watching.

"Barbones!" he yelled. "He-goats! Accursed liars! Let this be a lesson, fools! I know the wealth of every man here and either you pay or you pass by gunfire. Call up your women! Tell them to go home and dig! Here is the list!" And he stuck it to the wall.

Fox watched as the anxious wives came one after the other and read the names on the wall, and Maria was first of all. Pepe spoke to her briefly, she went hurrying out and a *mozo* brought the money behind her. Five thousand pesos! But the look she gave her husband was worth that or more to any man. Pizano accepted the payment, the iron gate clanged and Torres stepped forth a free man.

Other women came and paid, but Doña Luz was among the last. She entered doubtfully, her eyes on the burly guards who by now were comfortably drunk, then darted over to Gallardo.

"Shall I pay?" she asked under her breath.

"No!" he answered firmly as the crowd quieted to

listen. "They are determined to kill me, anyway. This is only a ruse, to have you lead them to the money, and then they will take it all. It is better for me to die."

"But Pancho!" she entreated. "Think of your family! Think of me! You can earn it back, after they are gone."

"It is too much!" he stormed. "Twenty thousand pesos for the mine, which has only been running a few months! I will pay nothing! I have no money hid!"

"Long Beard!" laughed one of the guards, "you are a great speaker—our General is listening. Now tell that lie over to him."

He drew back as Pizano came down to the gate and looked Gallardo over scornfully.

"So you have no money hid?" he repeated. "No treasure buried under the floor? Very well, if I find you are lying I will collect from you, two for one. Captain Gallardo!" And he raised his hand.

The door to his inner office flew open and a handsome young officer strode out. Don Francisco gasped—it was Bizco! In his broad Chihuahua hat and bandit rigging he had ridden into town unrecognized; but his sly, crooked smile and his mismatched eyes drew a curse from his father's lips.

"My son!" cried Doña Luz, rushing towards him; but he pushed her carelessly aside.

"No!" he said, "I am not your son. I have been disowned by this man here. But I have come back for my inheritance."

He rocked back on his heels and laughed as Gallardo stared through the bars.

"You are surprised, eh? You did not expect this? You

shall pay me, two for one."

He laughed again and Doña Luz rushed upon him, her agate eyes flashing fire.

"*You* are the one," she cried, "who has brought this upon us!" And she slapped him with all her strength. "Your father will never pay, if he dies for it!" she panted. "And *I* will never pay."

"No!" repeated Gallardo. "I will never pay."

Pizano stepped forward, his lip curled like a wolf's.

"You!" he said, pointing his finger at Fox. "Come out, I want to see you."

CHAPTER XVI

MONEY FIRST

L ISTEN!" began Pizano, fixing Fox with his crafty eyes, then glancing at Bizco Gallardo. "You know this old man, no? You work for him, in the mine. Do you know where his money is hid?"

Juan looked from one to the other, thought a moment and nodded his head.

"Ah!" smiled the bandit, "that makes it very simple." And going out he shut the door.

"That's fine," observed Bizco impersonally, still stroking the mark on his cheek where his mother's hand had struck. "Very fine for both of us, if you know what I mean. I suppose you want to live?"

"Sure!" answered Fox. "Why not?"

"All these men out in the Plaza are to be executed at sunset."

He pointed out the window to where eight frightened prisoners were surrounded by a heavy guard, and Don Juan glanced back at him questioningly.

"There was a little something between us," explained Bizco. "But I am sure you understand. With me it is money first. *My* money. Now where is it buried?"

"Under a floor down there. But this is not your money. I am paying it to save your father."

"No difference," shrugged Bizco. "I get half of it. A full half of everything I collect."

"Very well," answered Fox. "But tell me one thing. Would you let your own father be executed?"

"He is so stubborn—so obstinate," smiled Bizco. "I hope it will not be necessary."

"It will," went on Juan, "if you depend on him. He will never pay you a cent. But as his friend, and as manager of the mine, I am willing to go halfway."

"What do you mean—halfway?" blustered Bizco. "You are my prisoner—understand? I can put you in that gang and have you executed at sunset. Do you see anybody you know?"

"Yes. The two sons of Roque Salas."

"And Roque's brother! You see him too? That is for killing those two *gambusinos* and robbing the men at the mine. We are the friends of El Pueblo, the Common People, and *you* have robbed them worst of all!"

Bizco's eyes, which before had revealed only a slight cast, began suddenly to twitch and roll and he drew a pistol from his belt.

"Listen, Gringo!" he said. "I have you at my mercy. Now show me where that money is hid."

"Very well," agreed Juan—it was the only answer; and suddenly Bizco was all smiles.

"One moment!" he said. "You do not object to making a little money? We will take my father along."

"And why?" demanded Fox.

"Never mind," returned Bizco. "I wish him to be present."

And he motioned Juan out the door. Then he stopped for a hurried word with Pizano and shouted an order to the guard.

As he stood in the jail entrance Fox could see the Red Flag soldiers taking their ease in the plaza park. They were bearded, crude, weighed down with belts of cartridges and their eyes had a wolfish look. But they kept their horses close behind them, saddled and bridled and ready to ride. As for the rest of the scene, it was no more pleasant to him, for the Company store was being looted of everything and there was a fire in front of Castro's house. The aged miser's' cramped body hung stiff from the arch of his gate while his furniture fed the flames. Tables and chairs, rushed out by laughing soldiers and heaped up higher and higher. When Gallardo came out he looked once and turned away, and Bizco took another drink. Then he passed his bottle to the sergeant of the guard and led the way to the assay-office.

"Wait here," he said at the door. But the sergeant shrugged his shoulders in protest.

"General Pizano's orders were very strict, not to leave you out of my sight!"

"No difference!" snapped Bizco. "I order you to wait." And he slammed the door and locked it.

"Now!" he began, turning suddenly to his father, "you saw Castro, hung on his gate? That is the way we treat all *ricos*. But for you there is a way of escape. Tell me where the gold is buried at Miraflores! Make me a map and I will let you go!"

"No!" replied Gallardo, "I can read your heart. You are going to kill me, anyway."

"Then *you!*" cursed Bizco, drawing his pistol on Juan. "Where is this money? Show me the place!"

"It is here," answered Juan walking over to the wall and placing his foot on a tile; and Bizco motioned him on with his gun.

"Dig! Dig!" he rasped, "and if I find you are fooling me—"

"It is there," agreed Gallardo. "I know. But Juanito, you have made a mistake. To give these scoundrels anything is like throwing bloody meat to a wolf. They will only turn and devour you."

"I am sorry," began Fox, taking a chisel from the bench and prying up the brick; but Bizco cut him short.

"Dig!" he yelled, jabbing the gun into his ribs. "*Por Dios,* will you take all day? You are the man who brought this on me. Would I care too much if I killed you?"

He flashed his white teeth and in those twitching, beady eyes Fox could read his ultimate fate. Like a man digging his own grave for the firing squad, he would die when the job was done. Yet dig he must, and be quick. He had been tricked by Bizco, but his enemy had been drinking. There was a chance he might be caught off his guard.

Lifting out four broad tiles, Juan scooped up the earth and dug a hole against the wall. Their treasure was buried deep, so no tapping would reveal the cavity, and the chisel was his only tool. A wide, heavy chisel, capable of striking a terrific blow if Bizco but turned his head. It chucked against the top of the chest and Fox glanced up warily.

"Dig!" cursed Bizco. "Son of a Gringo dog, do you think I am not ready to kill you? Open up that box! Lift out the silver! Ah, *carai*—hear those devils at the door!"

The sergeant of the guard, who had been listening through the keyhole, had begun to hammer and thump.

"Open up!" he shouted and as Fox lifted out the bar of silver a new voice broke through the din—the harsh, vibrant voice of Pizano! In spite of himself Bizco glanced away and like a flash Juan was up and at him. One hand clutched the pistol and turned it aside while the other, still holding the chisel, slammed it down across his head. He struck again, the gun fell to the floor and Bizco went down like an ox.

"Come over here!" said Fox, grabbing Don Pancho by the arm and rushing him to the furnace door. "Here is *my* cave—I am going to hide you."

He moved a catch and the steel plate on the floor became loose after the first quick wrench.

"Jump down there!" he whispered. "Stay hidden until they go. If they catch you they will kill you."

"But you, Juanito!" protested Gallardo as he dropped into the hole. And Fox clamped the steel plate above him. There was no time to discuss the matter, for the outer door was swaying on its hinges. It heaved and fell forward and through the cloud of dust Pizano came charging in. He held a pistol in each hand and his face was working furiously, but when he saw Bizco he stopped short.

"What is this?" he asked, turning to Juan.

"Never mind!" laughed Fox. "Look at this!" And he pointed to the silver bar.

For an instant Pizano blinked, glancing quickly around the room as if searching for something else—then he ran over and looked down the hole. The guards came racing after him, a man reached into the box and brought up a huge sack of pesos, but as he whooped Pizano kicked him aside.

"Out of my way, *bribon!*" he cursed. "Where is Gallardo—that bearded old goat?"

The soldiers drew back, gazing stupidly around the room, still hardly believing he was gone. Then every eye centered on Juan.

"Where is he?" bayed Pizano, striding closer; but Fox only shook his head.

"Who knows?" he said with a shrug. "But there is the money for his ransom. Was not that the agreement, that for forty thousand pesos he was free?"

Pizano stared at him with unwinking eyes and then touched Bizco with his foot.

"And this man—who struck him?" he asked.

"I did!" answered Juan. "He was going to kill me." The General picked up Bizco's gun, which was cocked, and let down the hammer as he thought.

"Arrest him!" he barked. "Search the place for Gallardo. There is something mysterious about this."

He went back to the hole, snatching the treasure from the box while his men searched the darkened room; and as Fox, between two guards, stood looking on he wondered at what he had done. To save his own life he had struck down Bizco, although already he was beginning to stir. And then, to save his friend, he had thrust Gallardo into the cave which he had so carefully fashioned for himself. Now he stood unprotected in the presence of his enemies while Pizano regarded him intently. This outlawed bandit chief who made a business of robbing mines and hanging *ricos* from the arches of their gates! To rob and kill was all he knew and as he gazed his upper lip curled.

"Put him in with the rest," he said. "And at sundown—the *fusilado*."

CHAPTER XVII

THE *FUSILADO*

JUAN FOX, the adventurer, the Gringo, who had come south to spoil the Philistines, stood in the circle with the condemned ones and wondered what would happen next. He had overplayed his hand as an American citizen, and at sunset his light would go out. Unless, of course, he led Pizano to the hole and let Gallardo be killed instead. And even then they might execute him.

The old man had been right—to pay these bandits ransom was like throwing raw meat to a wolf. They had had their taste of blood and Bizco with his sore head was still waiting to shake him down. Waiting with gun in hand, but Fox had told him No. He had imbibed, without knowing it, the fierce fatalism of that land where every man knows how to die bravely when he stands before the firing-squad. If his hand but trembles as he lights his last cigarette he is no true son of Mexico.

But was it so easy, after all? Juan stood, a little dazed, with these miners who had worked for him and wondered how it had happened. He had certainly planned well when he came down into Sonora, selling sewing machines to raise a little stake. And he had played that stake well and earned more. He had even packed to go, but some trick of Fate had always stayed him—Elodia's handkerchief, her father's kind words. The old man had truly loved him, but the death sentence was the same. He had stayed too long in Mexico.

It was easy to see now that being an American citizen bought him nothing with this gang of outlaws. The Mexican Government, with which they were at war, would pay if anybody paid. Cruz Pizano had laughed when Fox had claimed exemption from the ruthless Law of the Gun. If Diaz could not get him with all his Rurales, what fear need he have of the Gringos? No, the thing for Juan to do if he wanted to live was to show where Gallardo was hid.

Every house, every store on that side of the plaza, had been searched by the trembling guards who had dared to leave him out of their sight; and Bizco for his treachery, his disobedience of orders, had been summarily reduced to the ranks. He, a captain of the band, to turn against his chief in order to get more gold! But before he had been struck down by Juan he had got forty thousand pesos, and for that Cruz Pizano let him live. For that and to find the Old Man.

That seemed a simple thing, too, as long as the Gringo lived, for he knew where Gallardo was hid. There are ways, as every bandit knows, of extracting such information. Ways handed down from Spain, passing on from father to son—ways that made the flesh creep, the eyes roll. But Pizano no longer trusted his captain's good faith—Bizco would keep the money for himself. He would hold the secrets as if they had never been told and then dig up the money for himself. But now they left Juan to think it over.

The sun was getting low, there was tumult in the square as drunken soldiers raced their horses to and fro; and in front of Gallardo's house a crowd of big-hat bandits was heaving furniture into the plaza. Then a pyre of black smoke rose up and they piled on more tables and chairs. The Day had come when the servant was greater than the master; but though they burned his goods Don Pancho still lived, and some day the Rurales would come. Perhaps soon—at any minute—the Red Flaggers were still watching for them. Juan hoped they would arrive in time.

He stood by himself, away from the other prisoners, but still under the guns of the guard, and now they began to joke him.

"*Oye,* Gringo!" called one. "When you die will you leave me those pants?"

They were the same Picacho Pants that he had won from Bozo Wilson, and Fox wondered if the Jonah still held.

"No, *Amigo,*" he answered grimly. "They are too

small for you."

"Then give them to me," urged a shorter one. "And for a favor take them off, before they are soiled with blood."

A roar of coarse laughter went up and as Juan glanced about he saw a face that he knew. A weak face, for all the fierce panoply of war with which the soldier had surrounded himself. It was Manuel, the brother of Bizco—he had been standing close to Fox for some time.

"You are ready to tell?" he asked, raising an eyebrow in the sly way he had. "The hour is getting late."

"No!" replied Don Juan, and turned his back on him. And yet, in a way, he was glad. In the uproar and tumult, the passing of bottles, the sudden affrays among the men, he might easily be overlooked and go to his fate with the rest. With Roque Salas's sons and his huge brother, Jose, one-time terror of all *gambusinos*. They had worked for the Company, opposed El Pueblo, and now they paid the price. But he, Juan Fox, knew where Gallardo was hid and was too valuable a man to let die.

"Do not make the mistake," went on the voice behind him, "that Roque Salas did. He laughed—he refused to believe. And then the *fusilado*—he was dead. Lead us to the spot where my father is hid and Pizano will give you half."

"No," shrugged Juan and at last, his anger rising, he whirled and faced his tempter.

"Sin-vergüenza!" he cursed. "Man without shame, would you send your own father to his death? I am only a Yanqui but I honor him too much to deliver him up to be robbed. These men here who guard us are ashamed to be seen with you—you father-killer, you Judas Iscariot!"

"Verdad!" joined in Jose Salas. "That is true, and I can say more. You and that base Bizco were *gambusinos* yourselves. That is why you have listed us to die. You not only robbed your father but the poor men who stole for you. Take shame! You are worse than a dog!"

"Shut your mouth!" retorted Manuel insolently; but at a loud laugh he slunk away. He and Bizco were no favorites with these rough Chihuahua bandits; and Cruz Pizano only kept them for a purpose. They had shown him a new country, where much treasure was hid; but in the pinch they had not made good. They had allowed Gallardo to slip through their hands and the matter could not wait.

A new guard, each man armed with a repeating rifle, filed out and surrounded the prisoners; and now the women of the doomed ones were allowed to say their farewells. There was weeping and sobbing, last kisses that broke the heart, and then they were put outside. But no one came to kiss Fox. He stood off alone, running his eye over the guards, watching the sun as it sank low in the west; and in his anger and hatred he promised to show them how an American chose to die. Not standing against the wall, lighting a cigarette for bravado, but fighting—fighting to the end!

One snatch at the repeater in the hands of some careless guard, a sudden whirl and rattle of shots, and as the Red Flaggers went down a rush into the plaza, a horse, and a dash into the sun. It was sinking now down the narrow street that entered the plaza from the west, and out that he would ride until he died. Died fighting—not shot down like a dog.

His face was tense as he watched the setting sun; and then, through the circle, a woman came running and threw her arms around his neck. It was Elodia—his Mariquita.

"My sweetheart!" she sobbed. "Are you determined to die? Have you refused to deliver him up? Ah, what a man, when his own sons have betrayed him! You are more than a son! I love you!"

The guards had become silent to catch this new drama and Fox played up to his part.

"Yes," he said. "I will never tell. Before I will betray him I will die."

"Viva!" cheered a drunk man and in the turmoil that followed she spoke quickly into his ear.

"Be ready!" she warned. "We will not let you die. When you see a black horse and a man that you know—"

"Enough!" broke in the sergeant, tearing her rudely away; and Mariquita fled through the crowd.

It was no fit place for a woman to be, and particularly a girl like her, but the great drama was drawing to a close and no one turned away to molest her. Then she was gone and Pizano came out with four *ricos* condemned to die. They had not paid their ransom, their friends had failed them, and they went into the circle of the condemned. Once more the wailing women were fighting their way through the guard, when up the street there was a clatter of hoofs.

Fox stood high to look—the horse was black! He set himself, and Yermo rode up. He wore a Chihuahua hat—but Juan knew him, and his purpose. It was a rescue. The horse was for him.

"Out of the way!" shouted Yermo to the crowd. "The Federals! They are coming. From the north!"

He galloped up to the jail door where Pizano was standing and dropped down with a proper salute. And then, through the guard, Fox bounded like a mountain lion. He landed in the saddle, and swung low.

"Kill the son-of-a-goat! He has stolen my horse!" yelled Yermo. And, snatching a rifle from a soldier, he opened fire down the street. The crowd scattered, the women fled, and in the dust at Juan's feet the bullets struck like hail, making a halo against the sun. They went past his ears like a flock of blackbirds; his mount stumbled, staggered sideways and missed his stride. Then, like the burn of a hot iron, a bullet seared Fox's back and he caught his horse's neck as he fell. There was a fusillade of shots, he splashed into the river and rode straight into the eye of the sun.

WAR

CHAPTER XVIII

PANTALONES!

THERE WAS A FURIOUS CHARGE to catch Fox at the river, but he knocked all the water out of the ford getting across and hit the trail north on the lope. Though the black was hit, he was still strong and speedy and he led the Red Flaggers from the start. There was a hole through one ear, his bridle was cut twice and he limped on his off hind leg; but he ran on untiringly, always hidden among the mesquites, until at dusk Juan reined him into a cow path. This broke into a wider trail heading west and, to throw off his pursuers, he swung up on the mesa and halted his blowing horse.

Hot and sweating, he dropped to the ground and ran his hand down the black's leg; but the wound was only a burn. The bullet had seared the inside of the hock, yet barely brought the blood. Fox could scarcely believe that his horse had passed through such a storm unharmed—and his own case was the same. A long rip across the seat of his Picacho Pants was the only injury he had suffered, that and a raw welt where the hot slug had passed.

He looked up at the sound of galloping horsemen and as the Red Flaggers hammered by below he called a curse on them and their kind. Something burned in his breast like fire and he felt himself strong with hate.

"To hell with you!" he yapped and rode west towards the far divide. They were raiders, killers, stealers of women, burners of towns—but too many for one man to fight. When he gained the pass and looked back he saw the flames in Todos Santos leaping high. Drunk and unrestrained, they were looting and burning, destroying what they could not use. And after this band would come more—and more!

"To hell with such a country!" he cursed and headed north for the American Line.

He had come south to spoil the Philistines and now they had spoiled him. They had stripped him of every-thing—his horse, his pearl-handled pistols—and left him a fugitive riding desperately through the night to save his own miserable life. His gold, his mine, his girl—all gone! But Gallardo, he was saved! He was buried beneath that steel plate before the furnace door. And with him was all the treasure that Fox had hidden away—his sacks of coin, his sheaves of currency, his bars of silver. All was lost, but it was probably for the best. If he had stayed he would have sacrificed his life.

It was a noble horse that Yermo had provided for him, and he and Elodia had forgotten nothing. There was a rifle in the scabbard, two belts of cartridges around the black's proud neck; and in the saddlebags jerked beef and tortillas, a bottle of mezcal, a double handful of gold! Good people, fine people, Guillermo and his sister. How prodigally they had wished him well as they sent him on his way. But the country—it was hell!

Fox took a big drink and turned his back on Todos Santos, Elodia, Don Pancho, everything! He rode down into an open valley where cattle were grazing and at every watering place he turned in, so that their feet would trample out his tracks. At last, towards dawn, he spurred up on a mountainside and swung back where he could watch his own trail; and if any Chihuahua bandit had the nerve to follow after him he was due for a quick trip to hell. On top of a flat boulder where he would not be seen, Juan laid out his saddle and gun; and below, near a spring, he tied the black, to be his watchdog while he slept.

The sun was past noon when, waking up from a sound sleep, he heard the horse jerk at his rope. Juan rose up softly and with rifle in hand peered over the edge of the rock. Yermo's black was snorting loudly, his ears were set and he was staring down into the valley. Fox followed his gaze and crouched back. Down the broad canyon from the north a long column of cavalry was marching, and every horse was black. They came on at a brisk walk in column of fours and, what he had not noticed before, there were scouts combing the slopes on both sides.

Juan reached for his saddle, slung his bridle over his arm and dropped down on the far side of the rock. These soldiers who marched in such perfect alignment, with guidons at the head of each troop, were Federals without a doubt; but did they come *por bueno o malo,* good or bad, for people like him? His buckskin trousers showed the rip of a bullet, there were two wounds on his horse—he flung on the saddle and was mounting to go when a shrill whistle made him look up. On the hillside above, two *vaqueros* were watching him, and both of them had guns.

"*Quien vive*—who do you cheer for?" they challenged; and Fox held up his hand for peace.

"For nobody!" he answered cautiously. "I am an American citizen."

They separated and rode down to meet him and Fox plucked his rifle from the scabbard.

"Who do you cheer for?" he demanded; but they did not give him a direct answer.

"Who knows?" replied the tall one; and reined in to look him over. "From where have you come?" he asked. "And where do you go?"

"From Todos Santos. I am heading for the Line. Who is in command of those soldiers down there?"

"Colonel Geronimo Beltran," announced the cowboy.

"Would you like to go down and see him?"

"Why not?" answered Don Juan promptly. "I have some news that may be of interest to him."

"Then ride ahead," said the *vaquero* politely. "We thought you were an *insurrecto*."

"No, indeed!" declared Fox. "It was their bullets that gave me this—and this!"

He pointed to the hole in his horse's ear and then at the rip in his pants and the cowboys burst out laughing.

"Which way were you going when you got that one?" asked the short man. "That is not the proper place, for a soldier."

"I think he was standing on his head," suggested the other. And once more they burst out laughing.

"If you had been where I was," retorted Don Juan shortly, "you would not find this quite so funny."

He mounted stiffly and, with his burned horse limping, rode slowly towards the column. Every eye was upon him as they advanced down the slope and, inspired by so attentive an audience, the tall *vaquero* began to shout witticisms. It was evidently a merry business, this campaigning with Beltran, and Fox did not begrudge them their laugh; but his face was a little red when he was brought before the chief.

Beltran was a tall man with a grizzled beard, and a black eye that looked him through, but he greeted Juan with a friendly smile.

"Do not mind these men," he said. "They are only volunteers. Is the army of Del Rio near?"

"Del Rio!" repeated Fox. "I know nothing of him. My troubles were with Cruz Pizano."

"Pizano!" exclaimed the Colonel; and suddenly his manner changed. "Be so good as to tell me more," he said; and while Fox described the raid on Todos Santos he listened in thoughtful silence.

"My friend," he said at last, "you have done me a great favor. I had heard that the Red Flaggers had been annihilated in Chihuahua, but they have only moved over into Sonora. We have swept this country clean without finding an army that would fight, but with Pizano it may be different. Can you guide me to his camp?"

"I could," answered Juan. "But I am going north. You will have no trouble finding him, especially with so many smart scouts."

He glanced at the tall *vaquero*, who had been lingering near, and Beltran dismissed him with a frown.

"You can leave in the morning," he said, quietly. "This evening you must be my guest."

"Very well, if you say so," replied Fox. "But I am determined to leave the country. I have lost all I have except my life, and this war is nothing to me."

"You are perfectly safe with us," Beltran assured him. "The Black Horse Cavalry is well equipped to protect you and I must hear more about this *bandido, Pizano.*"

"As you say," agreed Juan. "I see that my horse is lame, so I can rest him overnight."

"Not only that," answered the Colonel. "I will order him well fed and rubbed down. And you, *Amigo,* will stand some feeding, yourself. This fleeing takes the flesh from men's bones."

"And do the Federals never flee?" inquired Fox, sarcastically.

"No, Señor—they retreat. That is different. All my officers have been educated in the Military Academy at Chapultepec. They know the tactics and the rules of war. And my men! Each soldier has learned his duty. It would give us great pleasure to meet this Pizano."

"And it would give me great pleasure," said Juan, "to see him with a lily in his hand. Or is that the way you bury the dead?"

"Not exactly," returned Beltran grimly. "But if you wish to witness the battle you are very welcome to accompany us. You should see my soldiers in action, every man trained to do his part. They are not of this country and care nothing for these cowardly *revoltosos,* who are ignorant of the principles of war. Three to one or ten to one, it makes no difference to us. I have never seen the *pelado* that would face a machine gun, and we have eight, with millions of cartridges."

"But Pizano's men are all armed with repeaters," said Fox. "The bullets went by me like hail."

"One soon gets used to that," laughed the Colonel. "Not one out of ten thousand hits its mark. And my men with their Mausers can send a bullet twice as far. The repeater does well enough for hunting, but for military purposes it is worthless—it uses up too many cartridges. A clip holding five is the most used by any nation—and for that reason; but the seven millimeter Mauser has a bottle-neck cartridge, with smokeless powder and a copper-jacketed bullet, and its range is over two miles. Besides that, our soldiers are trained to stop and aim, to adjust their sights and make allowance for the wind. But these *insurrectos*—they shoot into the air."

He made the motion of emptying a repeater at the moon and called up his adjutant and supply officer.

"Go ahead to this next ranch," he directed, "and arrange to pitch camp for the night. We must locate this rascal, Pizano."

"Yes, sir," saluted the officers; and, when the regiment arrived, the camp-ground was already laid out. The guidons of each squadron were set in an orderly row and each troop halted on its line; then the men dismounted briskly, stacked their guns and unpacked their saddles and almost in no time the tents were pitched. Picket-lines were quickly stretched, the horses unsaddled and saddle-blankets spread out to dry. As for the Colonel, his tent went up as if by magic; and, seated in a portable chair, Fox looked on as the officers reported. Then scouts were sent out in the direction of Todos Santos and Beltran ordered up the wine.

"Your health!" he said as he raised his glass to Juan. "And do not think you are a prisoner. It is only that I need certain military information which no one but yourself can give. And you can identify Pizano if we kill him. But in the meantime you are my guest, and a very welcome one, for the life of a commander is always lonely. If he visits too long with this major or that captain the others take offense. It seems to them that he is playing favorites and discipline is broken down. So I am doomed to sit alone with my thoughts, and a civilian is more than welcome."

He poured out another glass and while they were taking their ease the striker served dinner for two. It was a very good dinner, for the foragers had combed the country for supplies; and at the end, seeing that Fox was interested in army life, Beltran sent for Captain Rodriguez.

"Take this gentleman around," he ordered, "and show him the different units of our camp. The packers, the scouts, the machine-gun troop. He has expressed a wish to inspect them."

"Yes, *mi Coronel!* With great pleasure!" saluted Rodriguez.

He was a small, dapper man, with his cap at a rakish angle and a rugged, devil-may-care smile; and when they began their tour he walked right past the cavalry until he came to the machine-gun troop.

"These are my men," he said. "My guns. The Colonel employs us for flanking. First we ride far around, our machine guns on mules, others following with boxes of cartridges. The enemy is occupied, they are lying behind lines, perhaps breastworks. No matter—we creep up close, we give them a burst, we jump them out of their holes. And then, when they run, we mow them down. They are whipped in a second. We are victorious!"

He smiled on his men and their faces lit up.

"It is very pleasant—very interesting," he observed. "But now you must see our scouts."

Fox followed, wondering vaguely at the naïve enthusiasm of this slayer-of-men. It was his business, his avocation, and he touched the guns lovingly—but the scouts were another breed. They were Sonora *vaqueros,* the best cowboys in all Mexico; big, rangy men, come along for the adventure and to kill the *pelados* who had been robbing them. Camped off by themselves they broiled raw beef on sticks or cooked tortillas on squares of tin, and did not even salute.

Instead, they laughed heartily as they greeted Don Juan and made remarks about the hole in his pants. He found indeed that they had named him *Pantalones;* and, after inquiring how he got the trousers, they asked eagerly about Pizano. Was he still at Todos Santos? Had his men burned the town? Would he advance still further into Sonora? Ah, what rascals! What barbarians! To line men up and shoot them because they had no money to pay! But wait! In the morning other scouts would be back and they would tell him news.

"Adios, Capitan! Adios, Pantalones! And be careful when you sit down!"

Going back Rodriguez stopped at the machine-gun troop again and ordered a unit to set up their piece. Then—as one rushed the tripod, another brought the gun and the others fetched out cartridges and belts—he went into a rhapsody of joy.

"This Pizano," he said, "will he stand up and fight? Del Rio is nothing but a coward. Perhaps if they join their forces we can induce them to engage in battle. Then, when our scouts have attacked them and they have formed a line to resist, we will ride around and come in on their flank. We will cut them off from their horses and when they start to turn—trrrrr! We will kill them in bunches."

"And what will they be doing?" inquired Juan.

"They will be running, flying, breaking their legs to get away—throwing away their hats, their guns! We live for the day when they will stand up and fight us! Did

Pizano have any machine guns?"

"Not a one!" answered Fox. "But he has repeating rifles."

"They are nothing!" laughed Rodriguez. "Those black-powder guns? Our *ametralladora* will shoot twice as far. We can mow them all down and never hear a bullet—would you like to see us do it? These bandits, these crude creatures with their big Chihuahua hats— what pleasure to see them fall! Only yesterday they held you prisoner—they took your horse, your guns, and con- demned you to be executed! But you outwitted them, you escaped!—And now for a fitting vengeance! Join our troop and be in at their death. You will laugh when you see them run!"

Something snapped in Don Juan's brain and made him see red.

"Will you lend me a couple of pistols?" he asked.

"With pleasure! Our very best! But do not miss this chance!"

"I will go then," decided Fox. And Rodriguez clasped his hand.

CHAPTER XIX

HUNGRY FOR WAR

DON JUAN slept uneasily, with dreams of sudden battles and Chihuahua hats falling like cabbage heads; and then at dawn a scout came galloping in with the news that the Red Flaggers had been found. They were camped down the valley, not five leagues away, and the Volunteers were waiting for daylight to attack them. Bugles blew, men rushed about, the horse-herds were brought thundering in; but after the excitement the Federals settled down to eat a belly-filling breakfast. This fighting was all in the day's work with them—let the Volunteers rush away if they would.

"They are full of hot blood," explained Beltran, smiling grimly, "and so I let them go. They hate these crude bandits who have been devastating their country and are determined to wipe them out, but their way of fighting is not war. Still it helps to consolidate the enemy and causes them to waste many cartridges, and, when my trained soldiers come up, perhaps the *insurrectos* will stand. And if by chance the Volunteers should be forced back that will lead the Red Flaggers into my hands."

He expatiated at length upon the principles of modern warfare as they sat at a very good breakfast; and then, with a leisureliness truly Mexican, the preparations for the battle were begun. Each separate band of horses was brought up to its picket-line and carefully saddled and packed. Then, loaded down with carbine and pistol and saber, with canteens and bundles and cartridge belts, the hardy little *pelones* mounted snappily and advanced in columns of four.

Excited scouts came galloping back with news of heavy fighting in which the Volunteers were getting the worst of it, but Beltran merely sent out observers. No bugle calls were given, he kept his Federals out of sight and soon the battle was close upon them. Down the wide valley, where single mesquite trees stood far apart on the white desert floor, scattered horsemen could be seen in retreat; and to the *pop, pop* of distant guns there was added the *spat* of spent balls and the whistle as they passed overhead.

Beltran halted his men behind the cut-bank of a sand-wash and surveyed Fox with a quizzical smile.

"Well, my friend," he said, "are you still hungry for war? Do you wish to have revenge on Pizano? Then join Captain Rodriguez and see for yourself how easily we defeat these barbarians!"

Juan dashed up the wash and soon the order came. Rodriguez was off, riding east. With scouts on both flanks and well in advance he turned at last to the south and, at a clean-cut volley in the midst of the heavy firing, he glanced at Fox and grinned.

"The Red Flaggers have charged," he said. "They have run into our trap. Now at last they know who we are and they take cover to save their horses. But wait till I come in on their flank and cut off their way of retreat. Then how they will run to get to their mounts! You will laugh—it will be your revenge!"

On and on through the tall trees they went at a fast trot, the machine guns and their packs to the front, the supporting cavalry behind. A scout came dashing back and they followed him to the right to dip down into a wide, sandy wash. Then they climbed the opposite bank and followed the stream-bed to the west, while the firing mounted to new heights. But through the sounds of battle the sharp volleys of the Regulars crashed like cannon.

"We are near them!" said Rodriguez; and at a turn of the crooked wash Fox could see the Red Flaggers' line.

Along the edge of the north bank a long row of Chihuahua hats nodded and bobbed as they rose up to fire; while beyond, under cover, their horses stood massed, held together by men with lariats. The battle was at its height, no one noticed Rodriguez's column, and he advanced within a thousand feet of the battle-line before he ordered a halt.

With a rush the gun-crews threw open their packs and lifted out the heavy pieces. One shouldered a tripod, another the gun itself, the third and fourth carried cartridges and belts; and, eight guns in a row, they scuttled through the brush and dropped down along the edge of the bank. They loaded, adjusted their sights, supported the breeches to break vibration and the Number One gun tried the range.

Put, put—put, put put! Down the wash his shots struck up the dust. Rodriguez stepped back smiling, his hand came down and the gunners opened fire. Along the bank where the Red Flaggers were gathered a huge cloud of dust was struck up; and out of it, just as Fox had dreamed, the big Chihuahua hats came tumbling down. A moment later their owners tumbled after them, and most of them were dead.

"Viva!" yelled the cavalry, crazy to charge in after the rest; but Rodriguez held up his hand. The gun-crews loaded new belts and waited and, just as the fugitives began to climb the south bank, a burst of fire mowed them down. It was a rout, a panic, a wild stampede; and the clearing dust revealed a long windrow of dead while the living scattered like quail. Then to the north a trumpet sounded the charge and Beltran's troops came

on at a gallop.

The Red Flag horse guards abandoned their herd and whipped away, following the dust of their comrades down the wash; and after them with sabers drawn the Black Horse Cavalry charged, slashing down every fugitive they encountered. *No quarter, no prisoners, no wounded,* was the motto of these grim fighting men; and on the heels of the first troop a second appeared, crossed the wash and went pelting on.

There were Red Flaggers everywhere, dodging like rabbits among the trees, frantic to find some way of escape; and with a yell Rodriguez's cavalry was upon them, pistoling every man in sight. Fox found himself in the lead, racing along beside the captain, and as they ran into a burst of gunfire he drew both pistols and charged. The Red Flaggers rose up shooting, fighting desperately to break the line and stave off their ultimate fate, but the cursing horsemen rode them down, knocking them over with bullets, until not a single man was left alive. Then, whirling, they were off and in the rush of battle Fox found himself as mad as the rest.

Had the Red Flaggers shown mercy when they rode into Todos Santos, killing and robbing in wanton spite? Had they spared the wounded, or the women who fled in terror? It was no more than their own code—no quarter, no surrender, no prisoners. A bugle blew and Rodriguez turned back, but Juan kept on after his enemies, emptying his pistols and reloading as he rode; until at last, turning west at a sudden burst of gunfire, he found the scouts closing in on a ranch.

At this place the night before the Red Flaggers had

made their camp, unconscious of the presence of Beltran; and in the morning at dawn when the Volunteers attacked, they had charged out and driven them back. But now the tables were turned and, hot for revenge, the scouts had resumed the assault. From the squat adobe houses a score of rifles spat fire; while the Sonorans, behind a cut-bank, circled their horses about, working their nerve up for a charge.

Fox rode in among them, a pistol in each hand, and as he looked around he laughed.

"Follow me, *hombres!*" he shouted, "this is no way to fight! You might get shot in the pants!" And he charged straight into the guns.

"*Pantalones!*" mocked the scouts; but, still laughing, they followed after him and the battle for the ranch-house began. Doors were smashed, horses went down, men fought hand-to-hand; but the Red Flaggers were beaten from the start. When the last of them, out of cartridges, came forth with hands raised the scouts shot them ruthlessly down. It was their code, their way of fighting—no quarter asked or given—and Fox accepted it along with the rest.

Beltran had asked Juan if he was hungry for war and at the ranch he received his answer. *Pantalones* had found himself, he had taken command of the *vaqueros* and captured the Red Flaggers' main camp. And in those squat adobe houses was half the loot of Todos Santos, besides all Pizano's supplies.

"My little captain," said the Colonel, "you have done well! And now you may go."

"Go!" repeated Juan, and Beltran smiled.

"To the Line," he explained. "You have led me to Pizano—"

"But I do not wish to go!" objected Fox.

"Very well," answered Beltran. "You are welcome to stay, then. God made you to be a soldier."

CHAPTER XX

THE ARMY OF EXTERMINATION

IN HIS BATTLE WITH PIZANO, Colonel Beltran had won a victory such as the people of Sonora had never heard of. Over four hundred Red Flaggers had been left on the field of battle and not a single Federal soldier had been killed. The Volunteers had lost eighteen men but hundreds more rushed in to fill their places, and for every recruit Beltran had a repeating rifle and a horse with a Chihuahua saddle. The whole horse-herd had been captured, guns and pistols were found everywhere; and the bodies of the dead had yielded jewelry and gold coins extorted from the peaceful *hacendados*.

The spoiling of Todos Santos—and of half Chihuahua, too—had been avenged in this one bloody fight and Beltran had won great renown; but his work was only begun. From the south, marching against him, a new army was coming on, the Army of Extermination. Over eight hundred Sonorans joined the Volunteers when news came of this army's approach, and when they heard that it was organized to exterminate them, the *pelones* rocked with laughter. A mob of *pelados,* half of them breechclout Indians, coming north to exterminate *them!*

Beltran sent his scouts out to supplant rumors with facts, but the "army" seemed no great menace. It was composed of Hot Country natives, still attired in their white clothes and broad hats, and its officers were untrained men; but Cruz Pizano and Del Rio had joined them and the combined army numbered over three thousand. All advancing for the express purpose of wiping out the Federals and thus striking a death blow at Diaz.

"They are fools!" scoffed the Colonel as he sat in his tent with Juan Fox. "The revolution is over. Before I left the railroad Don Porfirio himself wired me that everywhere the enemy was in flight. All that remains is to wipe out these 'armies' and restore a lasting peace. Then you, my *capitancito,* can return to Todos Santos and marry this girl you love. You can open up your mine without danger of interruption, and when President Diaz is informed of the service you have rendered, he will send a troop of Rurales to protect you. Until then you are my guest, and when we march against this army I will make you *cabo* over fifty scouts."

"Many thanks, *mi Coronel!*" replied Fox. "This business of war pleases me well. I have suffered enough from these ignorant *pelados* who march about eating up the country and at last am able to repay them. When the machine guns begin to mow them down all I ask is to finish up the job."

"Very well," nodded Beltran. "Captain Rodriguez will accept you as his support. And when his guns have put them to flight, these *vaqueros* will do their part. They are good riders, good shots, and with men like you to lead them will soon make very good soldiers."

"As for the rest," went on Juan, "my girl thinks I am dead and that is all for the best. I have no intention of marrying her. And if I return to Todos Santos it will be in the night, to dig up a little money I have hid. Then I will go back to my own country—but first we must kill this Pizano."

"But for him," nodded the Colonel, "I would have no fear of this rabble, though it is said they have two machine guns, besides a one-pounder cannon. But Pizano has been educated in war by fighting against trained soldiers in Chihuahua. We must be careful or he will play us some trick."

"I will never turn back," said Fox, "until I see him with a lily in his hand. And there are two other *hombres* that are as bad—one a cock-eyed scoundrel named Bizco."

"They are bad, these cock-eyed men," agreed Beltran. "Does Pizano never cross his eyes?"

"Only when he is angry—and then his men know the sign. A scout told me that for two days after you whipped him his eyes darted about like a snake's."

"Oh, well," observed the Colonel, "it is our duty to kill such snakes. Some say it is brutal to give no quarter, to pistol the wounded and execute the prisoners; but there is no other way with such men. They must all be wiped out, and in such a way that their death will be a warning to others. The common people must be kept down—they are in no way fitted to rule. That is reserved for the *gente de razor*—the people of reason."

He stroked his square beard gravely and proved beyond a doubt that God made the peon to serve; and his master, the good *Patron,* to rule him. And then, going further, he proved Madero a traitor for rousing the servant against his master. Fox had heard his views before and had listened tolerantly. Now he began to think he was right. Madero had planted dragons' teeth with his Liberty and Justice, and Mexico was now reaping war. Sonora was being watered with blood, and the tears of the mothers of men.

The Army of Extermination progressed but slowly, being busily engaged in looting every town and forcing the young men to join; and at last Beltran, having recruited his full quota of Volunteers, decided to strike the first blow. The country where he was was too brushy for the best use of cavalry so he planned to bring on a battle in a terrain better suited to machine guns. But now, after their first bitter experience, Pizano and his followers would be wary.

There would be no more blind rushes into ambushes, no more wild and unconsidered attacks. Pizano had learned his lesson and, since he alone was experienced in war, it was to be expected that his counsel would rule. But the weak place in the Army of Extermination was the horde of Indians who had joined, for they would never stand up against machine guns. So the great problem before Beltran was to get them out into the open and, after reconnoitering the ground for several days, he chose the place where he would fight.

It was a barren *malpai* mesa which rose above the bottom-land and extended east to the foot of the mountains, and the road over which the Exterminators must go trailed across it to avoid the floods. A heavy rain in the mountains had raised the river above its banks, making the lower road practically impassable, and while the weather was in his favor Colonel Beltran advanced swiftly towards the south. Before Pizano was aware of it, Beltran's scouts had occupied the mesa; and from its farther rim, with machine guns to support them, they put up a slashing fight. Then the well-trained little *pelones* began to dig trenches across the mesa, piling up blocks of lava to make three lines of breastworks from the river-bottom to well towards the mountain.

Bullets whizzed over their heads, the enemy machine guns opened fire; but the Volunteers kept the Red Flaggers to the lower ground until their one-pounder cannon opened up. Then, under orders from Beltran, they fell back to their breastworks, leaving the Exterminators to rush the heights. There was fighting across the open as Beltran retreated to the northern rim; and there he made his stand.

"Now," he said to Fox, "you may become a great soldier, so I will explain why all this has been done. The problem was to get the enemy into the open, where the machine guns could do their work from the flank, and for that purpose I myself built the three lines of trenches they now occupy. We are under the protection of the rim while the untrained troops of this so-called army are out on the level flat. They are under the delusion that their one-pound cannon has driven us off the mesa, but none of my men have been hurt. The retreat was to lead Pizano on."

He leaned over the portable table upon which he had plotted out his attack and explained the plan of action to his staff. Then with rapid orders he sent each officer to his post—Major Alvarez to the left wing with Rodriguez and his machine guns, Major Bracamonte to the right, while he himself commanded the center. The Volunteers were held in reserve to protect the horses, or placed behind rocks along the rim, and then suddenly the battle began. Thousands of cartridges had been fired on either side, Pizano had driven the Federals back twice; but Juan now knew that the crafty Colonel had only been leading him on.

As the machine-gun troop circled far off to the east, Fox could hear the volleys with which the Federal soldiers held back the enemy attack. Pizano's men were penned in between the rushing river and the cactus-covered heights and they were eager to break their way through. Every time the one-pounder burst a shell over the Federals they would give a triumphant whoop. But the men Fox did not hear were the silent Yaqui warriors who were slipping around to the east. There was a burst of fire ahead, a smashing of brush through the thicket and Alvarez's skirmishers came spurring back.

One flanking party had encountered another, but Rodriguez and his machine guns still pressed on. Major Alvarez remained behind with two troops of cavalry and a fierce battle opened up along the heights. Rodriguez looked back anxiously, sending more and more scouts to the right until at last he mounted the mesa. Then, unpacking his machine guns, he rushed them to the front to take the Indians on the flank.

With four men to a gun the crews stumbled across the open, taking shelter behind bushes and rocks; while behind them, dismounted, Rodriguez followed with the scouts, leaving their horses under the rim. The battle was moving towards them, bullets were flying overhead, and at an order from their captain the gun-crews set up their pieces and crouched down ready to fire. Then the white straw hats of a band of Yaqui warriors came bobbing from rock to rock and Rodriguez held up his hand. He waited until they rose and went bounding towards the rim, and gave the signal to fire.

Trrrrrr! went the Number One gun and the leaders fell in a heap.

There was a pause, the other Indians took cover; and then, as one man, they fled. Back towards the river and the trenches—and seven guns opened up on them at once. The path down which they ran became a windrow of kicking bodies, of tumbled hats and scattered guns; and in the panic that followed, the machine-gun crews snatched up their pieces and scuttled forward. Gathering others as they ran, the Yaquis dropped down behind the breastworks. But they did not understand the game.

Charges they knew, and ambush and retreat, but this flanking with machine guns was new. Fox could see them jump up as a burst of fire hit among them and then a volley of bullets mowed them down. And beyond them, down the trench, the Mexicans scattered wildly, taking shelter behind the next breastworks. But while all was confusion the guns were run up closer and Rodriguez dealt a final blow. He flanked the second breastwork, raking the trench its entire length, and the Army of Extermination was whipped.

Men lay in long rows, their bodies riddled with bullets; while the survivors made a dash for the third line. But they knew it was no protection, only a trap to line them up, and those that could kept on over the rim. Then a volley from Beltran took its toll and the "army" became a rabble, a mob. Guns were thrown away, men ran for their lives—for their horses, to mount and escape; but as they poured over the rim the Volunteers rode after them with wild, exultant whoops.

Once more Pizano's men found themselves cut off from their horse-herd and this time they knew what it meant. A long chase across the desert, harried like quail through the thorny brush, hiding desperately as bands of horsemen dashed past; and, for most of them, death. As the eight hundred scouts poured down on them they turned towards the river and ran. Some fell and were killed, some held up their hands, while others went down fighting. The rushing river saved the rest—that and the quicksands along the shore—but the "army" was a thing of the past.

At the head of his fifty scouts Fox dashed in to cut off the horse-herd; while, back on the field of battle, the disciplined Regulars rounded up the panic-stricken Indians. They lay hidden in blow-holes and narrow crevices in the lava, too frightened to attempt to escape; and as Juan came riding back he saw them lined up, to be cut down by machine-gun fire. There were peaceful Pimas and Papagos from the desert, who had been bribed with new guns to fight; and grim, swarthy Yaquis—on the wrong side again and destined to an untimely end. They stood in a long line, their heads proudly raised and as Fox passed a loud voice shouted:

"Patron!"

He turned his head quickly and, there with the rest, stood faithful one-eyed Fidel!

"Señor! Don Juan! Have mercy!" he cried; and Fox reined aside and stopped.

"Well, damn your black heart," he exclaimed. "What are *you* doing here, Fidel?"

"I was forced to join!" explained the Indian; and Don Juan slapped his leg sternly.

"Come here!" he ordered; and when Fidel grabbed his stirrup he started off on the lope.

"Halt!" shouted a sergeant, but Fox waved him aside.

"This is my *mozo,*" he replied; and Fidel ran beside him like a dog.

CHAPTER XXI

AMBUSH

THE RATTLE OF MACHINE GUNS as Indians went down before a burst of fire put a strange light in Fidel's one eye and he clung very close to Fox. The Federals were shooting them down in bunches, giving the wounded the *tiro de gracia,* piling the dead on huge piles of ironwood; but Fidel passed through it alive. Colonel Beltran himself gave the order that this one Yaqui be spared.

"To be sure, my *Capitancito,*" he said. "If this man is your *mozo,* that is enough. But to avoid any unfortunate mistake we will pin this on his shirt."

He wrote a few words on a piece of paper and turned to more important affairs. A great victory had been won, the one-pounder had been captured with all its ammunition, and the two new machine guns with theirs. The captured rifles lay in stacks, there was a great store of cartridges and the horse-herd would mount a thousand men. The *insurrectos* were in retreat, their flimsy army shot to pieces—but Pizano was not among the dead.

To make sure, Beltran had Fox walk down the lines of the dead, but the man they wanted was not there. Many a high-crowned sombrero lay on the breast of its former owner, who would never see Chihuahua again, and Juan scanned the swart faces hopefully. They had been a hard crew, these freebooters from over the mountains, and Pizano was the hardest of them all. He was a fearless fighter too, as long as he was winning; but at the first clap of disaster he was gone.

A black pall of smoke rose above the *malpai* mesa where the bodies of the dead were being burned and the Cause of the Revolution seemed lost. Del Rio had been killed and the General of the Southern Army, with Colonels, Majors, Captains by the score; but Beltran was not yet satisfied. Pizano was still at large—and the man who brought him in would receive a General's commission.

For fifteen years he had defied Porfirio Diaz to rout him out of his Durango mountains, but now he had been cut off. The mighty Sierra Madre lay between him and his old stamping-grounds, and the people here were unfriendly. The Sonorans hated the very language he spoke and every day more came to fight against him. Not *cholos,* not *pelados,* but the sons of honest ranchers whose estates had been laid waste by his horde.

The looting of Todos Santos and the holding for ransom of its citizens had been a warning of what was to come; and Pizano, even when he fled, took time to murder and rob. They were against him, these people of Sonora; and the news of the Colonel's second victory brought in hundreds of Volunteers. He sent them out in companies of fifty with some *hacendado* or *mayordomo* for chief, and their orders were to locate Cruz Pizano, then come back and report to Beltran. Meanwhile camp was moved, to get away from the battlefield, leaving burial squads to attend to the dead.

"My friend," he said to Fox when their new camp had been pitched, "take this Yaqui to be your striker. Since he must sleep at your door like a dog, make him your servant as he was before. But be careful—these Indians are treacherous."

"He is a man I can trust," stated Juan.

"Is he so?" smiled the Colonel. "Then call him in—I wish to ask a few questions."

Fidel came forward warily, that strange, scared look still in his eye, and Fox gave him the good news first.

"The Colonel," he began, "has said you can be my *mozo*. You can sleep here and guard my door."

"Many thanks," answered the Yaqui; and stood waiting.

"Your master," began Beltran, "is my *amigo,* my companion, and because I love him I have spared your life. But I wish to ask a few questions."

"Muy bien," replied Fidel without blinking.

"It was noticed after this battle," went on the Colonel, "that you Yaquis were all armed with Mausers—with

152

brand-new military rifles. Now who gave your people those guns?"

"Quien sabe," replied the Indian, after a silence; and Beltran glanced at Fox.

"Is this the man you said you could trust? Is he safe to have in our camp?"

"Seguro!" declared Don Juan stoutly. "But he is loyal to his own people."

"Perhaps so," admitted the Colonel grudgingly. "Now see what he will tell you."

"Very well," responded Fox and beckoned his *mozo* closer.

"Fidel," he said. "You saw these other Indians—these Pimas, these Papagos, these Yaquis. Someone had given them these guns, but do you think that man was your friend? Did he tell you that the Federals would mow you down with machine guns? Now all these Indians are dead."

He paused and an evil glint came into the Yaqui's eye.

"Sí, Señor," he said at last.

"That is bad," observed Juan. "The Yaqui women will cry. Many men will never come back. It is not good to believe all these Mexicans. They try to get your people killed."

"Sí, Señor," admitted Fidel.

"They will tell you anything to get you to fight. Did this man have a ribbon on his hat—red, white and green?"

"On his coat," corrected the Indian.

"When you went back to your people at Bacatete, how many guns did these Mexicans bring—a thousand?"

153

"Twelve hundred," answered Fidel promptly; and looked surprised when Beltran waved him away.

"That is all," said the Colonel, and shook his head at Fox.

"My friend," he said, "this is bad news for us. There is money behind this revolution—they are arming the natives against us. But if we can only kill Pizano—"

"We have got to!" declared Don Juan.

New scouting parties were sent out, all was ready for a start, and two hours after the news came that Pizano was moving south the army was on his trail. He had assembled his scattered Red Flaggers and, still up to his old tricks, was looting every village he passed. The towns were surrounded, their inhabitants rounded up and the merchants held for forced loans—and if any man refused he was executed. It was Pizano, beyond a doubt, and Beltran made a dash to catch him.

The Fox of Chihuahua had taken cover once too often—in the mountain town of Pino Blanco, where the Rio Puerco flows out of the Sierras, leading down through deep canyons to the plains. Before dawn the Federal army surrounded the place on the ridges; and when a machine gun in the tower of the church opened fire the captured one-pounder made reply. Only now it was being served by trained artillerymen, who burst their shells with perfect precision.

At the first shot the machine gun in the tower was silenced; and then, working fast, the gunners smashed in roof after roof until the startled defenders fled. For why defend a town when the enemy was out of range and this devil's cannon was sowing quick death? There was a panic, a stampede, a dashing of horsemen from street to street; and then suddenly in a body the Red Flaggers charged out and cut their way through the line. Pizano had seen he was whipped and, before twenty shells had burst, he had escaped before the trap could be sprung.

Beltran's cavalry went flying to cut off the Colorados, to force them to stand and fight; but they had gained the heavy cane-brakes along the river and nothing would rout them out. Major Alvarez crowded them close, they fought back viciously; and when a company of Volunteers charged after them a machine gun opened fire and cut them down. It was an ambush, as cleverly laid as any of their own, and over fifty scouts were killed. That checked the headlong pursuit and, with nearly nine hundred men, Pizano made a stand on the edge of a black brushy mountain.

For the first time since Fox had been with Beltran he saw him in a rage. His bandit enemy had outwitted him, he had turned defeat into victory, and along the mountainside the Red Flaggers were hooting. Yet the brush around them was so thick that no flankers could hope to penetrate it.

"Give me a machine gun," broke in Juan. "Sooner or later these Colorados will retreat down the river. With your permission I will lay an ambush."

Turning away from Major Alvarez, through whose line the Colorados had broken, the Colonel glared at him balefully. Then his lips twisted into a smile.

"Take two!" he rapped, and turned his back.

Fox called up his company of fifty *vaqueros* and started back the way they had come—and with them went two units of Federals with their machine guns packed on mules.

"Follow me, *amigos*," said Juan. "I will show you something to shoot at."

Circling clear around the black mountain, he cut the river below it, where the trail led on to the south. Down that way the Red Flaggers would retreat when the Colonel shelled them out of their stronghold, and every turn of the path offered an ambush. Against both canyon walls and wherever the water was still the cane stood in stiff, dense ranks; but at one place the ground was open. Digging in behind a log on the bank below, the two gun-crews trained their pieces on the trail and the long, long wait began. Their horses were under cover, the scouts were hidden below; and no one was to fire a shot until *Pantalones* gave the word.

He sat between the gunners and at last, from up the canyon, there came the clack of hoofs on the rocks. Then the leader of a pack train appeared and Fox and his men lay still. The mules stepped into the open, cocking their ears as they snuffed the wind, snorting and scrambling, looking up at the rocks; but at the curses of their packers they hustled by and plunged into the cane-tunnel below. There were thirty-one, all heavily loaded, and behind them came fifteen mounted men.

Their saddles were hung with plunder, with cartridge-belts, bandoliers; and, to mark them for what they were, each man had a wheat-straw sombrero such as only the Chihuahuans wore. And their horses! They were the pick of half of Sonora. Every saddle was embossed with silver and the horn was as big as a plate.

"Don't kill those horses!" whispered Juan. "Shoot the men off. Ready! Fire!"

Delicately, evenly, with the proud skill of trained men, the gunners opened with a burst and all fifteen riders went down. They lopped off over their saddles as if blown down by some strong wind, and the little *pelones* smiled.

"Good shooting!" nodded Juan. "I will report this to your Colonel."

Then, calling to the scouts, he ordered the pack train rounded up and the fifteen horses thrown into the herd. Not until the last animal was started back to camp would he allow them their soldiers' privilege of robbing the bodies of the dead. At any minute Pizano's whole army might come on them but, with the *pelones* in the lead, they rushed upon the fallen bandits and stripped them of their jewels and gold.

In some future ambuscade their own bodies might be as ruthlessly searched, but loot is the soldier's dream.

The sun was sinking low when they rode back into Pino Blanco, and when it was discovered that the packs held ammunition Colonel Beltran gave Fox the *embrazo*.

"My Captain!" he cried, "I appreciate your work. You have shown yourself a true soldier."

There were black looks from Major Alvarez and the other officers, through whose negligence Pizano had escaped; but from that time on Fox was addressed as *Capitan,* although he held no rank of any kind. He was merely the friend of Colonel Beltran, the American who always brought him luck, and this time he had turned the tide. Over fifty Volunteers, and good fighters all, had gone down before Pizano's machine guns; and, but for Juan's counter-attack, the morale of the scouts would have been shattered.

The country had changed as the army marched south until now the deep ravines, cut down through brushy mesas, made flanking almost impossible. They had come into a terrain where Pizano had the advantage, where every cane-brake became a potential ambush. The man who fled could lay trap after trap, leading his enemy up to the muzzles of his guns; and, but for one thing, Colonel Beltran might have turned back. Fox had captured the ammunition train, sent ahead while the Red Flaggers held the pass; and one more big battle would empty their cartridge-belts. But who would lead the way down that trail of death where already two companies had been wiped out?

Fox thought the matter over as he talked with Beltran, sitting at ease before their tent that night, and for the first time he began to have doubts. Carried away by the success of their first battle, he had light-heartedly thrown in with this old soldier to clear the West Coast of *insurrectos*. They had won, and won again; but now the country had changed and the gods of war had turned against them. From now on it would be brush fighting— plain murder from ambuscade with a sorry death at the end.

He pondered it well and reason told him to turn back— back to the American Line. He had proved himself a soldier and fed fat his grudge against the Red Flaggers, although Cruz Pizano still lived. Yet why bring on his own death trying to put a lily in *his* hand? It was a hard game that Beltran played, making a business of bloody death. Shooting his own wounded, lining his prisoners up before the machine guns! But when Juan tried to speak, the words stuck in his throat—he could not quit him now. Like a man in a dream he heard his own voice speaking, while his heart went out to his friend.

"Mi Coronel!" he said, "you have called me *Capitan*. You have honored me before your regiment and some of the officers are angry. I will show them before I go that I am a good soldier—I will take the lead, myself. And if this one-eyed Yaqui they all wanted to kill is brave enough to follow behind me, where is the Federal that dares to hold back? We will shame them! Eh, Fidel?"

"Sí, Señor!" responded the Yaqui. And so the die was cast.

CHAPTER XXII

ANOTHER ARMY TO WHIP

DOWN THE LONG, CROOKED TRAIL, scarcely more than a bear tunnel tramped through the heavy cane, Juan Fox led the Federal Army—the Black Horse Cavalry which had never been defeated and the Volunteers of Sonora. He led them out of pride and they followed from shame—yet brave enough, after all. One more blow and they would crush Pizano, but they had learned to be afraid of machine guns.

Once through this dark canyon and out on the plains

below they would have Pizano in their power. His army was dwindling down, every defeat meant more deserters, and now his ammunition was gone. Where in all this strange country could he look for more cartridges when his belts and bandoliers went flat? And then the people would kill him! They had suffered enough from the rapacity of his band—he would never reach Chihuahua alive. But before he could be cornered and defeated, some man must lead the way.

With Fidel close behind him, scanning the cane on either side, Don Juan rode his black horse down the canyon. He rode—to go out like a *caballero* if he ran into machine-gun fire! He would die on horseback, fighting. They would never call him *Pantalones* again! It was something almost glorious, to lead the way for these professional soldiers. And behind him, his stern face set, Fidel occupied the post of honor which no other man dared claim.

Mile after mile they fought their way down the canyon, where the muddy Puerco boiled over the rocks; until at last, beneath the heights of the two mesas, it opened out and the walls broke back. There was a wide space of bottom-land and, down a ravine from the west, a creek of clear water ran. Fox rode out into the sunlight and ducked, while his horse flew back with a snort. From the open space ahead a flock of vultures had flopped up, revealing a deserted camp.

Rusty buzzards with naked necks, *calele*-hawks with crested heads, leapt up with them and circled off; but the vile, frowzy vultures settled down on the first trees and regarded him with beady stares. Coming upon so many of these harbingers of death made Juan rein his horse out of sight. The Red Flaggers had disappeared but from any rocky point their machine guns might open up. It was a basin between high walls, heavily wooded with black brush—a natural ambuscade. In the shadow of a tree, as invisible as a wolf, Fidel scanned the slopes with his one eye.

"*No vale nada*—no good for nothing!" he pronounced; and the *Patron* nodded assent. Yet he had passed by so many ambushes, so many rustling canebrakes, that he shrugged and let his horse drink. All down the muddy river the black had snuffed at the water, but now he lowered his head and drank deep. From the dark canyon behind Juan's company of scouts appeared, rather shamefaced now that their danger was over; and *Pantalones* lined them up grimly.

"Now, *hombres,*" he said, "I have shown you the way down this canyon. Do you want me to lead you up that hill?"

"No, Señor," they answered, and laughed.

"Or perhaps," he went on, "you would like this breechclout Yaqui to show you how his people fight. We are soldiers, all, and no man knows the day when he will die. Is it not better to ride forward boldly and, if you meet death, go out like a man? You say yes, eh! Then scout out this basin and look for some hidden trap. For one man, or two, the machine guns will not open fire. Spread out then, but do your work."

They circled the edges of the big *redondo,* finding wide trails mounting up on both sides; but at the lower extremity the canyon boxed in, making it impossible for a horse to proceed. The Red Flaggers had ridden away several hours before, and apparently were in full flight.

"My Colonel," reported Fox, "the trails go up both ways but Pizano's men have turned to the west. There is no feed for our horses in this bottom—shall we take them up on the mesa?"

"Yes, my Captain," replied Beltran. "Wherever you lead we will follow. This hole is no place for cavalry. Lead up then and we will catch this Pizano."

"When we do," predicted Juan, "there will be Chihuahua hats thrown everywhere. But let me go ahead and find him."

"Very well—since you are so lucky. And take these glasses with you. But do not be too bold."

He unslung his fine field-glasses and gave them to Fox, who rode off laughing with his scouts. It was nothing to him if these Regulars became jealous. Let them take the lead themselves if they wished to be promoted. All he sought was the death of Pizano, and then he would head for the Line.

The trail of the Red Flaggers was trampled wide and deep where they had scrambled up the slope, and already along the path the scouts found pieces of plunder thrown away in headlong flight. At the end of their long trail the fear of death had come over them and they were stripping down to ride light. Still laughing, the scouts followed their *Cabo* at a lope, until at last they could look down on the plain.

It was wide, covered with giant cactus and thorny mesquite; and, down a road that followed the winding river, Juan could see Pizano's dust. The fear was in his heart—he was traveling fast—but off to the west where the highway ran there was another and greater cloud. Fox looked at it through his glasses and lowered them with a curse.

"Another army," he said, "heading north."

It was like a long snake, dragging its slow way through the thickets to come out on thinly covered flats; a huge army, but disorderly as befitted *pelados,* yet with close to three thousand men. Where did they all come from, these poor, benighted peons, to cast themselves upon Diaz's trained soldiers and be mowed down, mass after mass? From the blood of the slain a new brood of warriors seemed to sprout. Was it possible the revolution could win?

Juan sat down to watch them, moving north like all the rest—long lines of horsemen wearing Hot Country hats, following the phantom of Liberty and Justice. Knowing nothing they feared nothing—and each army was larger than the last. Some day they would overwhelm the Federals as armies of ants smother trenches of flame. Pizano was fleeing south, but he would cut this army's trail and come back as he had before. And then the extermination would begin—not a soldier would be left alive.

Beltran came galloping up to the edge of the mesa, but when he saw the new army he laughed.

"Poor fools," he said, "will they never give up? Here Pizano flees south and this other army marches north. We must destroy it before they meet."

He turned and rapped out orders, sending his Regulars ahead while the Volunteers were held in reserve. Troop after troop of Black Horse Cavalry poured down the slope and into the brush; and, from his position with the Colonel, Fox could watch every move that was made. One troop rode due west, to cut the line and rake the long road with machine guns; another circled north, another south, the rest came on behind. From his observation point Beltran directed them by signals, and he sent them in with a rush.

"Remain here," he said to Fox, "you have done enough for one day. Stay here and watch—you have the makings of a soldier, but I must show you how battles are won."

There was a rattle of rifle shots as the advance met the enemy and surprised them in the heavy brush, then the machine guns opened fire and a huge cloud of dust showed where the *insurrectos* fled. The black horses of the cavalry cut the road to the north, and a second battle began. They cut it to the south, dispersing the fugitives, and Juan hung his head for shame. He had counted Beltran whipped, overwhelmed by numbers, fighting bravely but against too great odds. Now he saw spread out before him like a picture the sure and certain way he dealt death.

From the hillside behind, a signalman waved his flag, conveying orders to the officers below, whose commands pressed irresistibly on; while in the distance, clouds of dust marked the *insurrectos'* flight or their fierce but futile counter-attacks. The sun was sinking low when he ordered a retreat and pitched camp near the river for the night. The Regulars rode back laughing, the Volunteers complained, but Beltran still held them in the rear. They must learn his sure advance and orderly retreat before he could use them in the brush.

As for Fox he was surprised that he had ever doubted the Colonel, ever questioned the decisions he made. With blows as swift and sure as those of a trained boxer he had driven the enemy in retreat. He had smashed this new army before Pizano could join it—and on the morrow he would smash him. He had plucked another victory from the knees of the gods and his soldiers were eager to go on. But in the morning from the heights the lookout saw Pizano riding north with all his men.

CHAPTER XXIII

THIRST

THEY RODE BOLDLY, these bandit-soldiers from Chihuahua, their round wheat-straw sombreros all a-glitter with silver, their saddles still hung with loot. Their flight had been stayed—they had located this new army, found a new source of ammunition and supplies. Once more they were headed north, ignoring the Federals who had chased them the day before. Beltran watched them through his glasses and his face went grim—he had educated Pizano until he feared him.

The battle that day began much like the other, with attacks in the center, flankers out on the left, the Volunteers fighting on the right. Rodriguez and his machine guns were mowing the enemy down when, far to the right, other machine guns opened up and the Colonel saw his Volunteers in flight. Big, cabbage-head sombreros rushed in savagely on their flank and the flight turned into a rout. Beltran signaled a retreat all down the line and made a stand on the edge of the hills.

It had come, the reverse he had feared, and Pizano had led the attack. He had taken a leaf from the old master's book and turned his flank by machine-gun fire. The Volunteers were badly demoralized and suffering from the heat of the day, when they rallied behind the Regulars, but just as the one-pounder was driving the *insurrectos* back another disaster broke. Riding down to the river to water their horses the fugitives ran into an ambush that made their panic complete. Machine guns, carefully hid on the opposite bank, opened up like the clatter-wheels of hell.

Beltran sounded the Retreat and, with his own men badly shaken, held the rear until the Volunteers reformed. He was cut off from the water—he was whipped. The army assembled on the summit of the dry mesa and, after shelling the enemy out of range, the Colonel turned back north. One man had defeated him— Cruz Pizano. What a pity, when he had had him in his power, that this new army should save him again! Three times he had routed him, and three times Pizano had escaped, and now he had an army at his back.

Beltran had lost men—more than he could stop to count for the horses were crazy for a drink—but as always they were mostly Volunteers. Between three and four hundred—and many wounded left behind to receive their *tiro de gracia.* Still, it was war and nothing could be done until the water at Redondo was reached. Major Alvarez was sent ahead, with six machine guns and the scouts, but through it all Colonel Beltran remained calm.

He had anticipated every disaster—save one.

As Alvarez and his troop reached the edge of the rim that looked down on the river below, the horses broke into a stampede. They knew the steep trail, and the water at its base, and nothing would hold them back. The soldiers behind heard the thunder of rushing hoofs—and then above their roar, the devilish chatter of machine guns. Only one man out of the fifty came back.

It was Pizano again, with the machine guns of this new army neatly ambushed on a point below; but the man who came back did not know. He stammered and made signs, his tongue dry for a drink, and Fox was sent ahead with his scouts. Then once more, like a waterfall that draws everything over it, the trail down to the water sucked them in. Juan's black fought his head, the horses behind went mad with thirst. Then they bolted, and Fox tumbled off. Some men stayed on, dazed, only to be captured and shot; while over the summit the rest of the horses poured, carrying their loads—everything they had. Even Beltran was left afoot—all the machine guns were gone. An army had been defeated by thirst.

It was dry, bone-dry, and hot. Every canteen was empty and men wandered about, distraught. Half their guns were lost and from the hell-hole below came the sound of machine-gun fire. And from the cane-brakes along the river there came the white smoke of repeaters, the bloodthirsty Red Flag yell! Pizano had repaid, he had fooled them at every turn, getting machine guns from no one knew where. All they knew was that every man of them would die unless Cruz was whipped from his den.

A dry camp was made on the mountain that night and

Colonel Beltran called a council of his officers. Their faces were grim and drawn, they held pebbles beneath their tongues to kill their thirst, and in every haggard eye there was death. Battling desperately all that day the machine guns had turned them back, but Beltran retained a semblance of calm.

"My friends," he said, "the fortunes of war have turned against us. We must capture those machine guns at dawn or every man in this company will die. One major has been killed, two captains, three lieutenants; but if we have the will we can win. Who is there that can take that point?"

There was a silence, and Juan stepped out.

"I can," he said, "if you will attack first down the river. All I ask is my pick of fifty men."

"And how," stormed a captain, "can *you* do this thing when our whole regiment has tried and failed? The Gringo goes too far with his crazy schemes. He will send us all to our death."

"All the same," answered Fox, "I have thought out a way and explained it to Colonel Beltran. But perhaps you can propose a better one?"

"Enough!" spoke up the Colonel. "His plan is good and I believe he can carry it out. I therefore appoint him major in place of Major Alvarez and ask you to pledge your support."

The young captains and lieutenants of Alvarez's old squadron stood silent in the presence of their chief. Even yet, while they were fighting for their lives and suffering the torments of the damned, they thought of promotion—of rank. Every captain had hoped to step into the major's place, and the lieutenants into theirs. But there was no holding out against the will of Beltran. They stepped forward, the captains first, and took off their caps. Then with a tiger look in their eyes, but smiling, they shook hands with Fox and promised him their loyalty and support.

The council broke up and Juan picked his own men for the attack—mostly seasoned *pelones,* each group under its own officers since to no others would they yield their obedience. And with them he took eight machine-gun crews to man the enemy guns if they were taken. Then, summoning them to a council, he explained his plan of attack, detailing every man to his place. Armed only with pistols they would creep up near the point where the machine guns commanded the canyon. There they would hide while Major Bracamonte led a party up the river from below. When the machine guns opened fire on them the attacking party would take the gunners from behind.

"Charge then!" he said, "and keep on to the guns or every man of us will be mowed down! Don't stop or we are all dead men. I will lead you and show you the way."

He dismissed them and lay down on the hard ground to sleep, but he could not because of his thirst. It seemed to burn like coals in the pit of his stomach, a gnawing pain that gripped his vitals and kept him awake. The others were the same, twisting and turning on their grass beds until at last Rodriguez got up. He stood for a moment over the place where Juan lay and touched him with his foot. Then he walked away and stopped.

Fox rose up and followed and the captain beckoned him on.

"My Major," he said at last, "there is something I must tell you. The other captains are not satisfied to have a civilian placed over them, and especially a foreigner. So do not lead the charge as you promised or they will shoot you from behind."

"Very well," agreed Juan. "But who, then, will lead?"

"These same captains," said Rodriguez. "I will stay with you in the rear and the first man that looks back—" He touched his gun.

"My friend!" exclaimed Fox, and shook hands with him in the dark. They went back and lay down together and long before the first dawn they were up. Nobody could sleep so the party was assembled and, barefooted, they crept down the trail. In the great pit below, Pizano's army was sleeping, dog-tired after their fight. There were twenty-five hundred men, with their horses and the captured horses of Beltran, corraled by the water below.

Juan led the way—following Fidel, who had the eyes of a wolf—and as the false dawn broke they saw the outlines of the point where the masked battery of machine guns stood. But outside the open trail the black brush was so dense that no man could see ten feet ahead. Yet the little *pelones* slipped through it until they halted not sixty steps away. Then, just at dawn, the machine guns opened fire—but they were shooting down the other side. At Bracamonte and his men, unwillingly playing the lure.

Fox raised his hand for the advance to begin, but he did not lead the way. He motioned them on sternly, his pistol ready to shoot—and the captains with the rest. *On, on,* he beckoned; and with his second pistol drawn he fell in beside Rodriguez. They were halfway up the point, not thirty steps away, before one of the gun-crew saw them. A lieutenant shot him down and they charged over the rocks while the guns on the summit still rattled. It was their favorite amusement, mowing them down—and they were in the midst of a cheer when the attacking party gave them a volley. Every pistol was out, every man went charging up and with a yell the gun-crews fled.

They ran down the hill but, when the *pelones* reached the abandoned guns, a different tune was played. A swift burst of fire cut the gun-crews to pieces before they could make their escape; and then, working grimly, the trained Federals swung the muzzles right into Pizano's camp. Eight machine guns were spitting at once and the camp disappeared in dust. Once more the big Chihuahua hats fell out of the smoke like cabbage-heads and the whole army started up the slope. On the opposite side, away from the machine guns, climbing madly to make their escape!

It was good to the Federals to see their enemies fall under the fire of their own abandoned guns, and when Rodriguez signaled back to the Colonel, Beltran charged down the trail with all his men. Bracamonte cut off the fugitives that started down the river and the killing in the *redondo* became pitiful. But not to the thirst-mad *pelones!* They charged in and halted, charged in again; passing up horses, loot, revenge; until at last the most venturesome knelt down by the creek and scooped up the water with their hands. Then they turned and ran back, snatching up rifles and full belts while their comrades rushed by for a drink.

When the carnage was over there were dead men

everywhere, especially along the brushy slope. And the loot! It was double what they had lost. They got back their own horses and those of the *insurrectos*—all their plunder, all their cartridges, their whole camp! By the fires that had been built the *pelones* roasted meat, boiled coffee, cooked tortillas. It was a triumph, a victory for the gods, and every man as he sped by laughed!

CHAPTER XXIV

ALL HELL

WAS THERE EVER SUCH A VICTORY against overwhelming odds? Beltran lined up his soldiers and, while the trumpeters blew *dianas* of triumph, he shook hands with all his officers. But to Fox he gave the *embrazo* and patted him on the back.

"My son," he said, "you were born to be a soldier." But Don Juan shook his head.

"No, *mi Coronel*," he answered. "I do not like this work at all. So I give you back my title of major."

"Break ranks!" ordered the Colonel without answering him; and with a long roll of the drums and a flourish of trumpets the band sounded the *diana* again. It was a pæan of victory echoing up to the heights where the beaten *insurrectos* hid, but Fox had had glory enough. The field of battle was a stench in his nostrils and he threw back into their faces the hate of his petty officers. No longer was he hungry for war.

"But my Colonel," he reasoned, "where will all this end? On one day you rout the enemy, shooting your wounded, executing the prisoners; and on the next day, they rout you, killing your soldiers from ambush, feeding their bodies to the vultures and buzzards. Is it necessary to hate so much? In a little while there will be no men left. You and I and all of us will be gone."

"Perhaps so," replied Beltran, "but to a soldier death is not unexpected. And in what way, but one, can it end? My command is thinning out—the machine guns have laid low some of my best. But can I surrender to these base *pelados?*"

"No!" said Juan. "The murdering devils would kill you—but no quicker than you would kill them. You are blood-mad, all of you, but this is not my war. I will find my pet horse and go."

"Very well," agreed the Colonel. "I shall be sorry to lose you. You have served me like a son. But you have earned the right to go. Look over all the horses, all the guns, all the loot, and take your pick of the best."

"A thousand thanks," answered Fox, "but my old horse is good enough and I see him there in the herd. As for guns, that is different. I will take two good American pistols, in place of those I lost at Todos Santos."

"Take the best," urged Beltran, "but do not leave at once. There are Red Flaggers scattered everywhere."

"Muy bien," agreed Fox and went to look at the pistols that had been stripped from the enemy dead. Ornate pistols, gold-chased, silver-inlaid, with handles of carved ivory, mother-of-pearl; and then, out of the heap, he snatched up his own lost ones with a steer's head done in pearl on the butt. His own guns, won back from the dead bandit who had stolen them! He unbelted and

strapped them on his hips and the Colonel nodded approval.

"Your own, eh?" he said. "It is a sign that you must go. Or do you believe in signs? In destiny, perhaps, like myself. I have no fear of death."

"I believe," answered Juan, "that a man can control his destiny. It is not necessary to stay here and die. But my Colonel, if you remain, trying to kill all these *pelados,* they will get you—there are too many of them. Have you ever asked yourself where all these armies come from? And where they get their guns? I hear that the Revolution is winning everywhere. More armies are always coming from the south!"

"So they are," responded Beltran. "With that I agree. But the Revolution cannot win. Have you not seen how my trained soldiers cut army after army to pieces? The Black Horse Cavalry is one of many regiments that serve Diaz all over Mexico. We are bound to conquer—it is our destiny—but to do so some must die."

He turned to the grim business of examining squads of prisoners before they were led forth to be executed. Of receiving reports on the dead and wounded and how many had received the *tiro de gracia.* Even his own men, too badly hurt, were shot with the rest. But they expected it, they knew no different. There was no surgeon, no medicine, no place where they could be cared for; and like their Colonel they expected death. But to be shot down like dogs, to be buried in the wilderness, to be left for the fowls of the air—that was something Don Juan could not stomach.

Fidel went running to catch the noble black, named

Yermo after his donor, and to hunt out his bridle and saddle. But Yermo whinnied eagerly—he was starved. All the horses had suffered for water on the day before. Now, down in this charnel-hole, they suffered for the grass that grew on the dry mesa above. Fidel hacked down some cane to feed him the tender tips and then Fox saddled up to go. Something told him to start that instant, but destiny intervened—the destiny that Beltran believed in.

First he ordered all the horses driven up on the mesa; and then, as a special favor, he asked Juan to view the dead. It was the same old quest—the search for his evil genius, Pizano. Beltran admitted it now—he was afraid of this uncouth bandit whom he had educated to be his peer. As long as Pizano lived there was danger on every point, death lurked in every cane-brake. He was a devil in human form, and his grinning face was not among the dead.

Fox could see the growing uneasiness of his Colonel as he glanced up the slope—that same rocky wall up which Pizano had fled, escaping the rapid fire of the machine guns. He was up there, watching, still up to his foxy tricks, still hoping to get back his camp. Scheming, perhaps, to stampede the horse-herd and leave them afoot again. Sending scouts out, barefooted Indians; naked Yaquis, with bows and arrows. Beltran posted guards—and outposts beyond them until they were four miles out from camp—one circled beyond another until he was satisfied. Then he asked Don Juan to remain.

Just for the night, for one brief visit. He was safer there than on the trail—with all the Red Flag fugitives heading north. It was a weakness that Fox had—he could refuse a woman anything, but not an old man. A trusted friend, like Gallardo or Beltran. But he kept his horse in camp. The air was electric with portents of swift disaster and he led Yermo up close beside him.

"I have a feeling, Don Geronimo," he explained. "It comes to me now and again and I find it better to yield. Whatever this prompting is, I know it is for my good. Do you never feel the presence of Death?"

"Always—and never," smiled the Colonel benignly. "He will take me when my time comes and not an hour before. But, down in this hole with these Indians in the hills, I can understand your fears."

"Call them fears if you will," answered Fox, "I am no longer an officer in your army. And when something tells me to go I will not stop to say good-by. You have taught me to be a soldier, but I do not like the game."

"Then ride where you will, my friend—I do not want you to die. We have been trained for different things and here our destinies separate. We will never meet again. And what a soldier I have lost! When this war is over and I report to Porfirio Diaz I shall inform him how you saved my regiment. No gift will be too great to reward you. But ah, if we had killed that Pizano!"

He sighed, glancing up at the eastern wall, and beckoned to his orderly.

"Recall the horse-herd," he said; and glanced at the wall again.

"Pizano!" he repeated. "He is my *bête noire,* my evil destiny. Something tells me he will strike again. For now he and his army are where we were yesterday—on the mesa, with no water, afoot. He is a wild man when he is fighting, but the bullets never strike him. Had we killed him I could be at rest. I would turn back to the north with my duty done, but I cannot leave him alive."

He rose up abruptly and began a round of the posts and Juan beckoned his *mozo,* Fidel.

"My friend," he said, "I have had enough of this. We are starting north tonight."

"Sí, Señor, " answered the Indian impassively.

"You are a good man," went on Fox. "You have served me well. But soon you can return to your people. Have you a woman at Bacatete? And children? They will be glad to see you back."

"Yes, sir," responded Fidel; and sighed. *"Mucho combate!"* he said.

"Too much!" replied Fox. "Always fighting—always killing. It is bad. We will both go home."

He reached into his pocket and brought out the gold coins which he had found still hid in his *cantinas.* Then he divided them evenly in his two hands and gave one half to Fidel.

"There is your pay," he said. "You are my servant no longer. When we leave here I will get you a good horse, a good gun, a pair of pistols. Is there anything else, Fidel?"

"Some clothes! Some good cloth for my woman!"

The Yaqui pointed to the uniforms that had been stripped from the dead and Don Juan nodded and shrugged. It was their way—they were all barbarians. But what a country—what a people to live with!

The horse-herd came pounding back to the water. The

soldiers cooked and ate—and slept. It was the time of the siesta, even Beltran nodded—perhaps also the outposts slept. And then, creeping up on them, came the black Yaquis of Pizano with their long bows and steel-tipped arrows. One by one the drowsy outposts went down, struck dead by the silent arrows, and Pizano's men crept closer. The great camp was still, only one man was awake—and suddenly Yermo raised his head. Fox watched him as he stared and was rising to look when a machine gun opened up on their camp.

Juan did not stop to look. He did not stop to think. With the first shot he leapt on his horse and headed up the trail. Then all hell broke loose at once and Yermo was hidden in dust.

CHAPTER XXV

DEFEAT

AT THE FIRST BURST OF FIRE, the first range-finding shots, every man in camp leapt up. Then it came, the volley of rifle-bullets, the rattle of machine guns—and the horse-herd broke into a stampede. Above the smash of lead Fox could hear them close behind, following the lead of Yermo up the trail; and the thunder of their feet drowned the yells of the Red Flaggers as they saw their enemies in flight.

Where they had come from and where they had got their guns was something to which Juan gave no thought. He lay low on his horse's neck and listened to the bullets going past. And Yermo! Did he know that sound and the bite and burn those flying slugs bore? The horses were stampeding but he beat them to the rim, and on over the mesa beyond. Then the herd boiled up after him and Fox headed them north. He circled them, slowed them down and swung them back.

Before, he had mounted and ridden by instinct, but now he was beginning to think. From somewhere Pizano had come back—with machine guns. He had returned with thousands of men. The hell's pit of the *redondo* was boiling with dust and smoke—boiling over with horses and men. These had survived, they had come through the storm, and as Juan circled back he heard the Colonel's trumpeter, sounding the rousing Rally Call.

Here was discipline, order, and in the midst of the rout the *pelones* halted at the rim. Colonel Beltran was there to command them, and when had their chief ever failed? Fox found him bareback on a frightened horse but deploying his men on both flanks, and he rode to the standard with the rest.

"On the left flank, Major!" shouted the Colonel. "Re-form your squadron! Return their fire!"

"Yes, *mí Coronel!*" replied Juan with a salute. But still his monitor told him to be gone. Why stay on forever, fighting forlorn hope after forlorn hope, when inevitably the end was death? Why fight these Mexicans' battles when at the first stroke of a bullet they would give him the *tiro de gracia* and leave him for the foxes to gnaw on? Yet he stayed, and in the lull he found Rodriguez.

His troop of machine-gunners had abandoned their pieces, being glad to escape with their lives, but they could not remain afoot. Catching any horse they could the more fortunate were helping the rest, rounding up the herd and roping out mounts.

"I saw your Yaqui," he called. "He was wounded. There he lies under that tree."

Rodriguez pointed, and with a strange sinking of the heart Juan hurried over to look. Fidel was down, there were blood-bubbles on his lips and a bloody spot on his right breast. But his eye sought out his chief's.

"*Patron!*" he implored. "Do not let them kill me. It is nothing!" And he tapped his chest.

"No! Nothing!" soothed Fox. "A clean hole through your lung. I will catch you a horse—we will go."

He galloped back to the herd, slapped his rope on a gentle mount and led him back to the tree.

"Do not let them shoot me!" repeated the Indian. "A Mexican was here. He looked at me."

"No!" answered Juan. "Did I not save you once before? I will take you away and cure you."

He dropped down and was binding up the wound when suddenly Bracamonte stood above him. Major Bracamonte, his senior officer.

"Look over there," he said. And as Fox turned his head he heard a shot. He looked back and Fidel was dead. There was a bullet-hole through his forehead.

"Mother of God!" cried Juan. "What is this? Have you killed my man?"

"To be sure," replied Bracamonte. "I gave him the *tiro de gracia.*"

"But you had no right to! He was my servant! My friend!"

"*No le hace!*" replied the Major, "—it makes no difference." And as he strode away he smiled.

Fox stood staring, first at him and then at the dead Indian and his eyes filled with sudden tears.

"Poor Fidel," he said, kneeling beside him; and as he wept Rodriguez rode past.

"My friend," he said. "Just a word. Be careful—the Major does not like you." Then he went on about his work.

"So that is it!" exclaimed Juan, rising up and mounting his horse. But when he came up to Bracamonte he was riding beside the Colonel.

"Come!" ordered Beltran. "There is a council of war. I am leaving the lieutenants with the men."

He set off at a gallop through the trees and, a full mile from the rim, called a halt. They were away from the sound of battle, the *pop* of copper jackets, the excitement of men rushing to and fro; and the Colonel, for one, was calm.

"My friends," he said, standing before them with his face towards the enemy, "once more we have met defeat. But the Black Horse Cavalry will never retreat from these *pelados,* though they come on a thousand to one. We will defeat them, yet—but first I must have your reports."

He stood there, erect and soldierly, a solemn glow in his dark eyes and Bracamonte was just beginning his report when there was a spat and Beltran fell dead. The dull spat of a bullet striking home—and its mark was in the middle of his forehead.

For an instant they stood staring, drawing nearer to look down on him, hardly able to believe their eyes.

They were beyond the range of fire but this one stray bullet, coming up from the canyon, had descended and killed their chief. It was as if the hand of God had smitten him, and in a panic everyone turned and was riding for his life. Beltran, the one man who could rule them, was gone; and with him went all order, all discipline.

Fox found himself alone in the presence of this friend who had always expected, but never feared, death. The bullet had come far, describing an extreme parabola from the bottom of the canyon to this spot, yet it had hit him in the forehead. Perhaps, after all, there was some such thing as destiny—when a man's time came he went out. Juan knelt down beside him as he had by Fidel, and once more it was Rodriguez who roused him.

"Up!" he shouted. "Up and away! If you stay you will not live an hour!"

He leaned down from his horse and laid a hand on Fox's shoulder, talking fast.

"Come with me!" he said. "Anything can happen now—the one man who could protect you is gone!"

There was a rush of soldiers from the rim and Juan joined in with the rest. They fled north, after the others, until a range of hills stopped them, holding them up as a dam checks a flood, and here Bracamonte gained control. Bugles sounded, men lined up, stragglers rushed to their commands and in the scramble Rodriguez disappeared. Fox threw in with the Volunteers, conscious of black looks from Federal officers which told him—for the last time—to go!

He spurred into a mass of fugitives from the rim and came across three *vaquero* scouts.

"Oye, Amigos!" he hailed. "It is time for some quick scouting, to find a way through these hills. Will you come with me? Will you ride?"

He jumped his horse into a lope, they fell in behind; he led the way, without looking back. These were honest Volunteers, Sonoran cowboys that he knew—no fear of them shooting him in the back. But Bracamonte!

He headed north. They rode fast. At a fork in the trail he sent two to the left and with the other took the right on a lope. The sun was sinking when they came to a second fork and Juan halted, extending his hand.

"Good-by, my friend," he said. "I am riding alone. Which one of these will you take?"

"This one!" grinned the cowboy, reining west. And Fox hit the long trail north.

THE AFTERMATH

CHAPTER XXVI

A DEBT TO PAY

THE HUSH OF EVENING was in the air when Juan gained the divide and looked back. Like all good Mexicans they had quit fighting at sundown, but at dawn they would begin again and Pizano would pay his debt. There was a faint bugle call—the Retreat—the Reveille—and Fox turned his face to the north. That was the last of all his enemies—all his friends.

They fought it out, there on the mesa, and the Black Horse Cavalry was annihilated. Like the splash of a stone thrown into a pond, the lost army was forgotten. They tried to cut their way out and Rodriguez was killed. They re-formed and stood against the horde until machine guns mowed them down, and the fugitives were captured and shot. Federals and Revolutionists, they lie on the mesa unburied, and there is nothing to mark the resting-place of Beltran or the vengeance of Cruz Pizano. A great wave of hate engulfed all lesser hates, while those who could, fled for their lives.

Juan led them by a night and hid out the next day, hearing rifle shots, seeing distant pursuits; but at sunset he rode down on an isolated ranch-house, his rifle across his lap. His hunger had turned him wolfish. Children hid, a woman came out, and each looked the other in the eye.

"Señora," he said, "I am hungry, but I mean no harm to you or your little ones. Have you anything to eat?"

"Yes, sir," she answered, speaking low, "I am expecting my husband back."

"No difference," he replied, "I have got to have that food. Set it out and I will pay you well."

"Sí, Señor," she responded humbly, and he led his horse up to the door. Then, holding him by the rope and watching the play of his ears, he ate until the table was bare. Children peeped out like mice from dark corners, the woman stepped often to the door. He ate the supper intended for four and left a gold piece to pay for it. It was more money than she had seen in years.

"Many thanks," he said, bowing low; and she watched him as he rode away. To the south! But when he was out of sight he turned around and headed north.

What a country! What a people! What all-engulfing

hate where no one could be trusted as a friend. And Juan had thought he was hungry for war! Now his Colonel was killed, Fidel was dead. He was hiding, a hunted man. Even the gold piece he had given the woman might bring the pack on his trail. He had money—gold—and they might try to run him down! But he had all night to ride.

There is a range of mountains to the south of Todos Santos and before dawn he was safe up a canyon—the same canyon where he had hidden from the Carillos, that time when they had sworn to kill him. It was a good place, because he knew the trails out of it, and he had dragged out his tracks at the forks. With Fidel to stand guard—but why think of it? Bracamonte had killed him. That was all the Mexicans knew now—to kill. Yet Juan had returned with a purpose, and he would not flee for the Line until he had dug up his treasure.

At the head of a box canyon, close under the limestone rim, a seep of water had formed and Fidel had hollowed out a pool. Fox rode in warily and when a deer jumped up he shot it. It was risky, but he had to have meat. Then as daylight came on he tied Yermo out of sight and mounted their old-time lookout.

Layers of smoke, hanging low along the bottom-land, marked the ranch-houses of humble Mexicans. Yet not so humble, either, now that the servant had been made greater than the master. With a gun in his hands every poor *paisano* had become overnight a warrior. And if, along the road, he should spy a Black Horse Federal with his loot still tied to his saddle—a fleeing *pelon,* a base slave of Porfirio Diaz—why then, the chances are he would kill him. Don Juan lay low, watching the dust as horsemen passed, looking long at Todos Santos.

Was he the man who, not six months before, had ruled that town like a lord? Was he Cabeza Colorado, the Manager of the famous Planchas de Plata that turned out a king's ransom every month? Then where was the silver he had dug from that hill and buried beneath the assay-office floor? Two mules could not pack it away if the looters had passed it by, and it belonged to the first man that found it.

But where was Don Francisco, that hearty old Porfirista who had defied Cruz Pizano to execute him? Had he lived—was it possible for him to live—with all these armies marching by? And what of the Señora and Yermo and Mariquita—Pepe Torres' madonna-faced Maria and smiling little Marcelina? Juan looked at the distant town on the hill and wondered what had befallen them all. Only a year before when he had come in from the north, he had found them living on happily, full of lusty loves and hates. Now a new year had come—and an overmastering hate that took no account of love and happiness.

Todos Santos was dark and still when Juan slipped into town, wrapped to the eyes in his blanket as he searched the empty streets for a friend. But every house on the plaza was dark, except one. There was a light in Pepe Torres' *cantina,* and the sound of rough voices inside. Fox listened for a moment and hurried on. His friend Pepe was not there. There was nothing left, not even the familiar houses that looked out on the park. They were burned down, blasted, laid in ruin by dynamite. The church tower had fallen to the ground.

But the treasure—was it still in its hiding place? Juan

circled through back alleys until he could peer into the doorway, and the whole assay-office was in ruins. The floor had been dug up until nothing but pits and mounds marked the spot where his furnace had been. What frenzy of greed had spurred them on to this? They had found his treasure—it was gone! He passed out silently, keeping close in the shadows, for a fight had sprung up in the saloon. Chairs and lamps were being smashed, men were running to and fro. One was down—many more were upon him.

With his heart sick from it all, Juan hurried back to his horse. He would start for the Line and never stop riding until the sun drove him back into the hills. But as he untied Yermo where he had left him in a thicket there was a clatter of hoofs down the road and the black burst into a whinny. Fox grabbed him by the nose, another horse answered, then the posse of Mexicans swept past. Peering out Juan saw heads against the sky, and in the midst of them a single man—bound.

The cavalcade passed on, down the road to the south, and he heard a voice that he knew. Loud and hectoring but with a timbre all its own. It was Bizco—Bizco Gallardo. Fox had almost forgotten him in the rush of greater hates, but as he listened something stirred in his breast. Bizco, eh? He had sold his own father. Bizco the cock-eye, who had brought back Pizano to help him rob his home town. Who had shoved a gun against Juan's ribs, waiting to kill him when the treasure was dug up.

He swung up on Yermo, who fought his head to follow them. But no, there was death that way. There was a hanging, a garroting, some foul form of murder; some private vengeance on an enemy. Fox reined towards the north but Yermo champed the bit—he was back home and Bizco's horses were his mates.

"Well, go on, then," muttered Juan; and they went loping down the road. A flash of memory had come over him. That man in the mob, the man bound tight with ropes—he was Apolinar Lopez, the gambler. A little man, but nervy; it was a shame to let him die. Fox reached out suddenly, caught Yermo by the nose and pulled him down to a stop. He had heard the horsemen ahead—they were turning off up a canyon.

For a long time, out in the brush, man and horse fought their battle; but Fox had a hackamore and he won. Every time the black filled his lungs to neigh, Juan cut off his wind with the rawhide. And then the posse came back—whipping, spurring, racing each other to town, while Juan held fast to his mount and choked off each feeble wheeze. It was Bizco, it was Manuel—and Yermo was a Gallardo horse.

He jumped, he bucked, he backed into the thorns; but Fox spurred him until he came out. Then slowly, quietly, he turned off up this canyon where Bizco had stayed so long. It was necessary for Juan to find out what had happened to Apolinar, his friend. Something moved in the deep shadow of a tree and Yermo almost jumped out of his skin. Fox dropped off and tied him fast—that something was Apolinar.

From his head to his feet he had been bound to the tree by a band of green rawhide, newly skinned; and already it was cutting off his breath. Juan whipped out his butcher-knife and slashed the rope away and Apolinar fell on his face. Then he turned on his back and sighed, feeling his throat until his voice returned.

"Mother of God!" he gasped, suddenly sitting up and staring at his friend. "Who are you? Or am I dead?"

"No," answered Fox. "I am Cabeza Colorado. You are safe."

"But did you come back from the dead to save me? We all know you were killed by Pizano!"

"Not quite killed. I escaped and have been fighting ever since to lay him out with a lily in his hand. But no difference—let them think I am dead."

"But you are not!" declared Lopez, cocking his head to one side. "I can see those same Picacho Pants that you won from Bozo Wilson!"

"They are the same," admitted Juan. "But come—let us leave this spot before these garroters return!"

"No!" cried Apolinar with sudden vehemence. "I have a debt to pay. And since you are my friend I will borrow your butcher-knife. This very night I will strike, when they think Apolinar is dead."

"Very well," agreed Fox, "but before you go please tell me what has taken place. Where is my old friend, Don Francisco? And Pepe Torres—is he dead?"

"He went back to Spain in time and saved his wife and family. But Don Pancho remained and, right in his own house here, they tortured him until he died. It was another army of Red Flaggers, and his wife got to town too late. She would have dug up the money to save his life. But when she saw him dead, and her son Bizco there, she fell down and passed away in two days. Young Yermo was impressed into the Army of Liberation. And

Elodia—she disappeared. So it is with all the people we knew—they are dead or have disappeared. Just as you, my friend, disappeared."

"I have come back with nothing," confessed Juan, "and the first man that sees me will kill me. But you I know I can trust, so I will take you to my hiding-place."

"No, no!" protested Lopez, struggling up, "I have a debt that first must be paid. Now, while they are drinking at the bar! While they think Apolinar is dead! First Bizco, and then his brother, and then those low *cholos* who all leapt on my back at once. We were gambling, Bizco and I, and in a game there is supposed to be honor—the code of a gentleman—but I won! Ah, false-hearted, cock-eyed scoundrel, I will pay you at last! Let me go!"

"To be sure!" returned Fox. "But where will I find you, since here you are my only friend? I must ask you more questions before I leave."

"Ah! About the treasure you had buried beneath the furnace! It was found—by this same rascal, Bizco! In three days after you had hid him Don Pancho reappeared as smiling as if nothing had happened. But Doña Luz would never be satisfied. So he told her—and in some way Bizco heard. He went back and dug up the floor."

"It is gone, then," sighed Juan, "and I am stripped down to nothing. Very well, I will leave the country."

"But no!" protested Lopez. "You have not asked of *me*. Between friends, then, I have turned *bandido*. What difference if a man wears one ribbon or another? They are all bandits—all robbers at heart. Some take all your property and give you a receipt. I take it and give you nothing. Join my band, Don Juan—you are a man I can trust—and not all this treasure has been dug up."

"Well—perhaps," said Fox, not to hurt his feelings. "But no man must know I am here. I am considered to be dead and dead I will remain. I will show you my hiding-place."

"No, no!" cried Lopez. "These *garroteros*—you forget them!"

"They can wait," answered Juan. "I will take you to my cave and you can meet me there—if you live."

"I will live!" replied Apolinar grimly. "I will live to bury this knife in every assassin's heart and wash my hands in his blood. I swear it—I will kill every one! But since you are my friend I will spare you a little moment. Get your horse, then—we will go to the cave!"

CHAPTER XXVII

BETWEEN FRIENDS

IT WAS THE SECOND DAY. Don Juan had been hiding until his meat had run out and his patience had come to an end. Why wait any longer for this bandit, this crazy man, who had gone out to kill nine with a butcher-knife? Apolinar Lopez had said he would come back and there must be a reason if he failed, since he was known to be a man of his word. Very well, then, why not face it? The gambler had tried and been killed.

Fox caught up his horse and saddled to go, but a dust down the road held him back. It came out of Todos Santos and at the fork of the trail a single horseman turned off. He was elegantly mounted on a prancing bay steed, his saddle gleamed with silver, but all the same it was Apolinar. He came straight up the canyon and when he met Don Juan he handed him a bloody knife.

"Many thanks, my friend," he said. "They are dead and will trouble honest men no more. But it is rumored about town that a strange horseman has been seen, so I came to warn you to go. A man on a black horse, bearing the brand of Gallardo—it would be unfortunate if someone should meet you."

"Yes, unfortunate for him, for killing is no novelty to me. I have seen men shot down too often."

"You are a man I could well use," observed Lopez. "Have you considered my offer to join?"

"I have indeed, Apolinar. But tell me a few things first. I have been cut off from all news for months. Has the Revolution triumphed?"

"So they say," responded the bandit, "but the price of bread is the same. Men ride about robbing and shouting for Liberty and only one thing is certain. Porfirio Diaz has been deposed and Madero is President of Mexico."

"Is that so?" exclaimed Juan. "I can hardly believe it. And what brought all this about?"

"Don Porfirio was growing old, his enemies rose against him, and so the aged lion was dragged down. His teeth were too blunt to bite."

"And Madero? What sort of a man is he?"

"A good man and honest—so they say—but he is a pacifist, not believing in war. The peons are all free but there is no one to direct them, so nothing has been planted in the fields. All the old *hacendados* have been killed or driven out and the country is going to ruin. The only ones who prosper are men like me and my band. The Revolution has taught us to steal. We are all robbers, now—the poor against the rich. And soon there will be no rich."

"A sorry country," said Juan at last. "And so my old friend, Gallardo, was killed?"

"Killed for his money. But the greatest treasure of all was never found. When Doña Luz died the secret died with her—where Don Pancho had buried his gold. It is known that his father hid hundreds of thousands of dollars in the ground. It was French money—*louís d'or,* they were called—and what a sight it was to see Bizco and Manuel begging their mother to reveal its hiding-place. She had suffered a stroke but could talk if she would. But no, she saw through them at last. Poor woman, if she could have lived to see me stab them to the heart and send their black souls to hell! And now, although she is dead, her spirit still haunts the spot. Miraflores is where the French money was buried, but no one cares to dig there. Unless you would like to dig?"

"Not I!" declared Don Juan. "There is a curse on the money. And since you have asked me a question I will ask another of you: Why am I such a fool as to stay in this country, suffering the torments of the damned, in order to kill more of my enemies? I believe I am just plain crazy, so I am going back to the Line."

"Very well, my friend," sighed Apolinar. "I had hoped you would join my band; for the rest are a little *bruto;* a little rough. But if you will go it shall not be on that black horse, for the first man that sees him will kill you. It is his rider who is believed to have killed nine men and the whole country hereabouts is aroused. So I will give you this bay, the best horse I have. Take him, and go with God!"

"My friend," said Juan, "I thank you for this offer and I shall always remember your kindness. But the black was a present from Yermo and Elodia, and I will keep him for their sake. Has nothing been seen of her, you say?"

"Nothing for months. She left town in time and took shelter at the ranch, and when her mother died she disappeared. Perhaps she has crossed the Line."

"Perhaps so," nodded Fox. "If I had known what was to happen—but no matter—show me the trail."

"Up the sand-wash," directed Lopez, "and keep clear of Miraflores. Men have died there—the trail has been changed. Also Mal Paso—do not cross it before dark. Good luck, then—I owe you my life."

"You owe me nothing," said Don Juan, "if you keep this a secret. Let it always be believed that I am dead."

"I promise," responded Apolinar, kissing his thumb in the Sign of the Cross. "But here is one little thing I had forgotten."

He unwrapped a package from his saddle and displayed a fine pair of *charro* trousers.

"A present," he hinted. "And, since you will have no further use for them, I will take those buckskin pants in their place. The ones you won from Bozo Wilson."

"A thousand thanks!" cried Juan. "They are beautiful! Wonderful! And these I have are becoming old and frayed. Can you ever forgive me if I ask to retain them?

I have sworn an oath to wear them across the Line!"

"Excuse me! I had forgotten!" exclaimed Lopez. "Here are a hundred pesos in gold. It is just that I like them. Something about them. They are the pair that you won from Bozo Wilson."

"Yes, indeed!" smiled Fox. "But you have forgotten all the bad luck that goes with them?"

"I am *muy hombron*—all man!" declared the bandit. "I will take a chance on all that."

"No, *Amigo!*" laughed Juan, "you are afflicted enough to have to live in this God-forsaken country. So indulge me, as a friend, and for saving your life. I cannot give you bad luck."

"Very well," agreed Apolinar with a gusty sigh. "Go with God, then. I wish you well!"

He waved his hand in salute and Fox galloped off down the trail. It took nerve to deny so much to a friend who had just killed nine men with a butcher-knife.

A little early in the day, since others were abroad, but boldly riding his black horse, Juan Fox started north for Mal Paso, which was best not crossed until dark. But Yermo champed his bit and fretted, being on the road towards home, so at first Juan gave him his way. But at the fork below Miraflores, where a sand-wash led up to the house, he jerked his head towards the north. Yermo jerked back, fighting the bit, snuffing the wind and trying to neigh; but men had been killed in the lane by the ranch-house and Fox gave him whip and spur. Then they went on more slowly and at every cow path Yermo tried to turn to the left.

Toiling up out of the heavy sand, they gained the old

trail at last—that same deep-worn highway down which a year ago Don Juan had led his train. Sixty mules, loaded with sewing machines to sell to the Mexicans—and now he came back broke. Broke and worse than broke—a fugitive from war—a marked man, hunted to be killed. He had won much and lost much, escaping with his life but having nothing but bitter memories.

Over the brow of this same mesa he had halted at Miraflores, selling Elodia her sewing machine. And in stopping to teach her he had fallen under her spell. She had been beautiful, his Mariquita! But he had steeled himself, resisting her charms. Now she was gone and all the rest were gone—the war had taken them away. All was lost, the orange had turned to ashes. There was no love, no happiness, in Sonora; and on this trail the bandits had had their way. Piles of stones, leaning crosses, signs and symbols of sudden death! He drew his gun out and laid it across the saddle.

The way grew rocky, the giant cactus tall and gaunt, the thicket bristled with spines; while across the path the slender wolf's candles hung their blood-red lanterns in the dusk. It was that time of evening when the darkness would blur a man's sights, and yet the sun still lived in the west. It had set, but behind San Lázaro there hung a nimbus such as surrounds the heads of martyred saints. An evil omen to one who believed in signs. But Fox did not—he sheathed his rifle and drew a pistol for quick work—and at that moment a gun blazed in his face.

Bang! it roared, from behind a rock ahead; and Juan ducked as Yermo whirled. He was ambushed. He swung low and raked with the spurs. Then *bang,* it barked again and something hot ripped across his ribs. Only a burn, a scratch, but as he hammered down the trail he felt the blood on his shirt. Just a wet place to which the cloth stuck. The old musket whanged again but the assassin had failed—Mal Paso would not have a fresh cross.

There was nothing to do now but ride back, and go out over the trail to the west. And that was a way he had traveled only at night, into a country he did not know. Back into the desert where he had met Beltran and gone south with the Black Horse Cavalry. He muttered to himself as he clattered down the highway. Would he never reach the Line? Must he always be turned back by the muzzle of a pistol or a gun belching fire in his face? And him a marked man, riding the big, black horse whose owner had killed nine men. Apolinar had hung his crime on him—between friends, since he was heading north—but now it had gone past a joke.

Juan reeled and clutched at the horn, then pulled Yermo down to a walk. He had gone faint—his brain had whirled. It was his wound—the blood running out. Holding tight with his knees he felt along his side, cursing weakly, feeling the sop of his shirt. Out in the open trail, with the wall of cactus on both sides, and no place to stop and bind it up. His brain whirled again and he came to holding the horn. It whirled yet again and he woke up at a gate, where Yermo raised his head and neighed. Then a fierce dog came rushing out, Juan's horse flew back and he landed on his face in the dirt.

CHAPTER XXVIII

FOR LUCK

A VERY HARD-LOOKING MEXICAN with a gun in his hand stood over Fox when he came to himself—and yet he seemed familiar. But Juan had seen so many bad *hombres* he could not remember them all. The muzzle of the gun he recognized.

"Where did you get this horse?" demanded the *paisano,* swinging a candle; and Fox blinked his eyes and sat up.

"What horse?" he inquired, to gain time.

"This black, with the iron of the Gallardos on his hip. Speak quickly—did you steal him?"

"No, no!" denied Juan, fumbling furtively for his pistol; but the Mexican had taken his guns.

"Outlaw! Bandit! Highwayman!" he raged. "You are the pig's son who has been murdering everybody. In Todos Santos, *bandido!* You are the man on the black horse!"

The muzzle of the big pistol moved closer to his forehead and Fox drew back with a start.

"Be careful!" he warned. "There is more than one black horse. This was given me by Yermo and Mariquita!"

"And *who?*" inquired the man, looking closer; and at that moment a woman shrieked.

"Stop! Stop, Pascual! It is my Redhead! My lover!" And from the gloom Elodia rushed out. She struck away the gun, snatched the candle and held it closer, then knelt down and clutched Juan to her heart.

"My sweetheart!" she sobbed. "Have you returned from the war? Have you come to save me from this death? Put that gun down, Pascual! He is hurt!"

"But he stole our horse!" objected the Mexican. "He is the man on the black horse who killed your two brothers. He is a bad man and should be shot."

"Oh, 'shoot, shoot'! That is all you know. Everyone that rides by you would kill. But this man—no! He is Cabeza Colorado! Help me lift him—carry him into the house!"

"'Sta bien,'" grumbled the servant, catching Fox by the shoulders; and with a great shuffling of feet they bore him in and laid him down on a bed. Then Elodia leaned over, holding the candle, and looked Juan in the eyes.

"Aren't you Redhead?" she asked, her voice breaking doubtfully. "You are so different—and yet—"

"Yes!" answered Fox. "But where am I? At Miraflores?"

"Yes! Yes! It was our horse that brought you back. But you are wounded—there is blood on the bed!"

"Take me off, then," he said. "I was ambushed at Mal Paso. It is only a scratch up my side."

"It is a wound!" she cried. "A terrible wound! Pascual, let him lie where he is!"

"But, Señora, he is bloodying the bed!"

"No difference!" she stormed. "Can't I get this through your head? He is my lover—there is nothing too good for him!"

"'Sta bien!'" replied Pascual. "But have you considered this? He is the man who killed your two brothers!"

"Were they so good, then, that they should never die? Did they consider their poor father—their mother? He is welcome to this house, whoever he has killed. Go away—I will not have you around!"

She turned on him so wrathfully that Pascual slunk away and she slammed the door behind him. Then she ran over and knelt by Juan.

"My lover!" she sobbed. "My prayers have brought you back—I could not believe you were dead."

She kissed him, bathing his cheeks with her tears, but Fox only struggled feebly.

"Fix my back," he complained; and fainted.

Far into the night he was conscious of her, working over him, and of stinging medicine that hurt his wound; but it was something else that was wrong.

"I'm hungry," he said at last; and Elodia uttered a scream.

"Oh, my Redhead!" she cried. "Will I never learn anything? In a little moment you shall be fed." She hurried away and a few minutes later she brought him hot coffee and goat's milk.

"Now a drink of mezcal," he ordered robustly. "Or a bottle of that old cognac."

"You need food!" she advised; but she poured him out the cognac and for the first time that night Juan smiled.

"*Salud!*" he muttered as he emptied the glass; and once more Mariquita burst out weeping.

"I love you so!" she sobbed. "Can you forgive me for forgetting? All I can think is—my lover has returned!"

"But badly shot," he mumbled. "What's the matter

with my head?"

"You fell off your horse when Carlos rushed out at you. And Pascual was going to kill you—he drives everybody away."

"A bad *hombre!*" pronounced Juan. "Bring me my guns."

And when she found them he dropped to sleep.

In the morning he was sore, his wounds were stiff. He did nothing but eat and rest. The next day the same—his mind seemed a blank—and Elodia left him to himself. She had much to do and, over her sewing machine, Juan could hear her singing a song. Always singing, always sewing—but now her clothes were somber black. Her father and mother were dead. And, for that matter, Bizco and Manuel, though she did not speak their names. All her family were dead except Yermo and he was off to the war.

What a country! Fox was crazy to be gone—to get where the trails were safe and no highwayman would shoot him down. It was bad luck for him—twice he had turned and fled and both times he had been hit from behind.

"Bring me my clothes!" he ordered; but Elodia shook her head.

"You are better off without them," she said. "Perhaps tomorrow, if your wound has healed."

"But I want them!" he demanded roughly. He had learned a rough way in camp.

"They are being mended," she answered; and came over to feel his brow. "I believe you have a fever," she went on.

"No difference!" he shouted. "I want my clothes."

"My sweetheart," she said, sitting down on the bed, "do you remember when you nursed me? When I was bitten by the terrible *matavenado?* It was said at that time that the sick one must obey, and now I am nursing you. You are very thin—many days you have starved. Stay with me and get back your strength."

"But my enemies will follow and kill me! All I think of is to get across the Line!"

"You must wait," she answered mysteriously. "This highwayman may shoot you again."

"So he may!" agreed Fox, "but I am going to do your country a favor when I leave. I am going to kill that man."

"Ah, my poor Redhead!" she sighed. "Is that all you do now? Always fighting—always killing—always at war? Then think of us poor women who can only look on—or perhaps run and hide from the soldiers. It is terrible! Have you noticed how I look?"

She brushed back the hair from her face and with a pang he noticed the wrinkles.

"I am an old maid now," she said.

"No, no; my Mariquita!" he soothed; and for the first time since he had come back he kissed her. It was true, though—her beauty had fled. That vivid, flashing beauty that had made his senses reel! And yet—there was something else.

"You are pretty enough," he said.

"Oh, do you think so? Do you like me? Perhaps it is this old dress!"

"You look better in red," he decided. "What is that you are sewing on all the time?"

"I will show you!" she cried. "But no—it is not done. Would you like to shave your beard? We are getting old now—we must look our best, you know. You can shave while I finish my dress."

"Very well," he answered and as he watched her dart away she seemed suddenly to have become young. What hateful clothes these Mexican women wore—a widow's weeds when they had passed their first youth! The little maidservant brought hot water and a razor and held the glass up before him, but when he looked into it he paused. Was this the man he had come to be since last he had shaved his beard? He was haggard, thin, grown old before his time—and in his eyes that look of the wolf! He shaved away the beard but the look was still there—it was sinister, malevolent, ferocious!

He gazed into the mirror again and glanced at the little girl. She was the same pop-eyed creature who was always staring at him, and now her eyes bulged from her head.

"Well," he said, "what's biting you?"

"Nothing," she answered, and looked away; but the glass began to tremble violently.

"I look very ugly, eh?"

"Sí, Señor," she replied; and he laughed.

"Well, what is it?" he demanded at last.

"With permission, are you the man that killed Bizco?" So that was it! He told her no.

"And Manuel?"

"No. Yo no!"

"And the seven other men—at Todos Santos?"

"You have been talking to someone!" he accused; and

Elodia came hurrying back.

"Go!" she said, "I will wash his face, myself." But in the midst of it she stopped and kissed him.

"I am glad," she beamed, "that you did not kill my brothers. Pascual has been telling her tales."

"It is nothing," he answered. "Is the dress done? I want my clothes!"

"In a minute!" she soothed. "But do not be surprised. I have made a little change. Do you believe in bad luck, Juanito?"

"No!" he stated impatiently. "But I will if this run keeps up much longer."

"Then you will be pleased!" she said and danced away. When she returned she bore a pair of fancy trousers, which looked a little small. "These are for you!" she observed and smiled, but Redhead's eyes bulged out.

"I want my old pants," he rapped.

"I am sorry—they are gone," she answered. "The bullet cut a great hole."

"Then mend it!" he cried in his rough way.

"But I could not, Juan. Another bullet had hit there before. Don't you think they are very bad luck?"

He gazed at her, astounded by the look in her eyes.

"Where are they?" he asked at last.

"With permission, I burned them up."

"What?" he yelled. "My Picacho Pants! I was just offered a hundred pesos for them."

"Then you should have taken it," she said, and laughed. "To get shot twice in that same place is bad luck."

He glared at her a moment, then reached over and took

204

the other pants.

"I made them, myself, on the sewing machine," she offered. "I will retire, while you try them on."

Don Juan looked at them a while and laughed shortly, then he rose up and put them on.

"By grab," he muttered, "there may have been something to that!" And as he strutted about Elodia returned. But not the same Elodia—she was the Mariquita of his dreams, the ladybird who brings good luck. All red and brown, with black spots on the wings, and she danced over and gave him a kiss. That was two since he shaved off his beard.

"My sweetheart," she said, "you look so young again since you shaved and put on these nice pants. Shall we take a little walk in the garden? Very soon I must let you go. But not with those terrible *pantalones*. Think of all the bad luck they brought. And to Bozo Wilson—and that man before him! Don't you really believe in signs?"

"Never mind," he replied, "they are gone. And now, with these on, I can go."

"Yes, yes; to be sure. But tell me—is there nothing in these signs? Do they not, in some way, control our destiny? I prayed for you while you were gone, and the good God has brought you back. Do you remember the Gypsy who told me my fortune? She said you would come—from the north. Ah, how I wept when you told me they were horse-doctors! People who stole chickens and robbed clotheslines! Look, here is the very spot!"

She pointed to the stone bench where they had sat out their brief moment of love, and Juan drew himself away.

"Ump-umm!" he said, "if I should sit there again—and

with you wearing this dress—"

"It was wonderful! I shall never forget it. All the doves in the palms, the little birds singing, the flowers—just like today! Only now it makes me sad. Have you never noticed how sweet a thing is if you view it with eyes of love? But when you are unhappy, when everything is lost! I do not like this place any more. And the Gypsy, she was so honest—she described you so perfectly—I cannot disbelieve her yet."

"It *is* strange," admitted Juan, sitting down on another bench, "that I should come to you again, and from the north. I was leaving the country when this cursed highwayman—but never mind, I will pay him back."

"Please do not, my Juanito!" she begged. "Some day a bullet may kill you. And then whom can I think of, sitting here all alone, if my sweetheart is forever gone? Is it nothing, what I have suffered to win your love? Must you leave me to mourn your death? I do not complain, I know you do not love me, but leave me something to cling to. You do not understand this terrible lovesickness which has wasted my beauty away."

She touched his hand hopefully but his wolf eyes gazed straight ahead.

"I will tell you something," she said, "since you do not believe me, since you think these are nothing but words. That terrible *matavenado* that bit me—I went out and caught him, myself."

"And let him bite you?" he demanded.

"So I would belong to you," she smiled. "I loved you so much, but you never came. And I remembered little Marcelina. They all told how you cared for her, how her parents had given her—"

"No, no," he broke in. "Do not tell me any more. I am weak now—we must go inside."

He staggered as he rose and she helped him in. Then he lay there, thinking, until dark.

"Bring my horse," he said. "I must go. But some day I will come back."

"No," she corrected. "You will not. But *muchacho,* get his horse."

The boy went running and Pascual appeared, to speak in low tones to his mistress.

"You need not fear the pass," she said to Juan.

"Pascual has killed them both—the two highwaymen who waylay people there. He is always wanting to shoot someone, so I told him to go and kill them."

"You are bold," replied Juan. "I like a brave woman. And some day, if you wait, I will return."

"Not for me," she said. "I must die an old maid. *Adios!*" and she offered him her hand.

"*Adios,* then," he replied. "But walk with me to the gate—and tell these staring people to go."

She dismissed them with a look and faced him defiantly; and in her presence he stood abashed, saying nothing.

"Elodia—Mariquita," he began, "I did not know I had hurt you so much. I did not know how I had made you suffer. Will you kiss me now—good-by?"

He held out his arms and she flung herself into them. Her hot kisses stung his lips.

"Oh, I love you!" she sobbed. *"Adios!"*

"Love me still?" he asked, turning back.

"I love you always," she said and bowed her head.

"Then, my ladybird, my sweetheart, I will take you along for luck. I am broke, I have nothing, but when we get to the Line I will marry you before the Judge and the Priest. You are my woman—you belong to me."

"Mi corazon!" she cried, and wept. "My Juanito, have you saved me from this living death? Have you saved me from being an old maid? Then I have something else we must take."

She opened the door to an inner room and lifted up a tile.

"It is the gold of my father," she said.

"Now give me another kiss!"

Center Point Publishing
600 Brooks Road • PO Box 1
Thorndike ME 04986-0001 USA

(207) 568-3717

US & Canada:
1 800 929-9108